FAMILY SECRETS

By

John S. Bartolotta

BOOK WRITING
P I O N E E R

Author's Bio

Born in NYC to a large Italian American family. He worked as a meat cutter with his father from a very young age. Drafted into the Marine Corps in 1966. John is a Vietnam veteran, wearing many hats through his years from plumber owning a small business, becoming a real estate Broker, and a career in labor relations. Retirement stimulated a talent in art. Painting, sculpture and wood carving featuring his work in many art shows. In spare time he began writing short stories and metaphors which were well received encouraging him to publish Fina The Trilogy. A fiction thriller full of twists, turns, romance, thrills, chills and surprises and Fireside Tales. A collection of chilling tales that keep you wanting more. Both are available on Amazon Kindle Books.

Dedication

Dedication I dedicate this book to My Christine

Without her support and encouragement

It would not have happened.

She is amazing.

Thank you My Love,

For coming back into my life,

Freeing me to create these pages.

Acknowledgement

I want to thank my family and friends that have read and critiqued my stories, edited and liked them as well as appreciated and favored them. Motivating me to publish them.

I will always be grateful.

Table of Contents

Chapter One

In a mansion located in Newport, Rhode Island, resided the estate of Sir Andrew Van Cleese, a fourth-generation real estate tycoon with vast holdings in millions of dollars' worth of real properties. Sir Andrew passed away at the age of 96, leaving behind a legacy of cantankerousness, overbearing behavior, and obnoxiousness. His vicious tongue and cruelty towards staff and business associates had left him isolated and lonely.

Surprisingly, his only heirs were five nieces and nephews whom he had never known. These children were the offspring of his brother Bernard, who had been banished from the mansion after being discovered in a sexual relationship with a black housekeeper named Evette Geoffrey. Bernard had fathered five children with different women: Filomena Kudrow, Beatrice Fargo, Grace Winslow, Carmella Price, and the aforementioned Evette Geoffrey. Unfortunately, Bernard had not provided support for his offspring. He was known for his philandering ways, dishonesty, ruthless business practices, and struggles with alcoholism. His life ended in his 40s, marked by loneliness and a lack of love, as his various mistresses were forced into the role of a single parent.

Evette, the daughter of Bernard and a black housekeeper named Evette Geoffrey, raised her son Timothy. Timothy went on to marry and have a son named Winston, who eventually married and had a daughter named Simone in Ohio. They led a modest family life, and Simone struck out on her own at the age of 18. She moved in with two other girls and began working as a waitress at a local restaurant. Simone was a striking young lady, known for her beauty with big green eyes and a petite frame that concealed her surprising strength, as she held a second-degree Black Belt in Tia Quan Do.

She enjoyed a generally happy life with many friends but had not yet found a remarkable man. However, her life took an unexpected turn when she received a letter about her Great Grand Uncle's passing, summoning her to the reading of his will. This was a surprise to her, as she had known nothing of his existence.

Trey Wilson, a 30-year-old gambler primarily engaged in Texas Hold 'Em, was a free-spirited, nomadic individual. His financial status swung wildly, going from having more than enough money one day to being broke the next. He was a tall, good-looking man with wavy brown hair, dark eyes, and a charismatic personality. Always carefree and on the lookout for a game and a woman, Trey's lineage traced back to Carmella Price, one of Bernard's concubines. Calvin's daughter, related to Carmella, had married Ed Wilson, and they had a son named Trey. Trey had a tough upbringing, frequently finding himself in trouble. Skilled with his fists, he began making money through prize fighting as he grew older.

His life took a turn when he found himself in a high-stakes card game one night and emerged as a big winner. Hooked on gambling, Trey moved to Las Vegas to continue his thrilling lifestyle. Receiving the letter about his Great Grand Uncle's passing was exhilarating for Trey, akin to winning a significant hand in Texas Hold 'Em.

Lester Coonz, born to Roger and Leslie, was a Realtor operating in Chicago. He partnered with his father, Roger, in their realty business, primarily dealing with residential properties in and around the city.

Bernard, on the other hand, had an affair with Filomena Kudrow, a dancer in the Follies, during his younger days. Bernard was infatuated with Filomena; her beauty was undeniable, and he spared no effort to attend her performances. He lavished her with wining and dining, taking her to all the most renowned restaurants and clubs in town. However, everything changed when Filomena informed him that she was pregnant. Bernard abruptly left town, severing all contact with her. Filomena's son, Jeremy Kudrow, later became the father of Lisa, who married Oscar Coonz, Lester's grandfather.

Lester himself was a ruthless businessman who didn't hesitate to sell homes to individuals who couldn't afford them, only to foreclose on these properties when the buyers defaulted on their payments. The letter he received about his Great Grand Uncle's passing only fueled his insatiable greed for money and power.

Giselle Tweed was raised in the lap of High Society. Her mother and grandmother were prominent socialites, regularly mingling with the rich and famous.

Bernard's path crossed with Beatrice Fargo at a fundraiser held in honor of Senator Philip Kearn's re-election campaign. Beatrice's captivating charm and extravagant personality immediately caught his attention, and he was enchanted. His charisma and substantial wealth proved irresistible to her. For nearly a year, they were inseparable, with Bernard lavishing her with gifts ranging from precious jewels to a luxurious apartment overlooking the park. However, their blissful union took a drastic turn when Beatrice revealed her pregnancy, which prompted Bernard's hasty departure, leaving her with an opulent apartment she couldn't afford and a young daughter, Giselle.

Giselle enjoyed a privileged upbringing, attending elite schools and living a life of luxury in New York City. Unbeknownst to her, her mother faced financial struggles, relying on influential acquaintances to get by. Eventually, Beatrice orchestrated a marriage between Giselle and Martin Tweed, a stockbroker on Wall Street. Tragically, three years into their marriage, Martin suffered a fatal heart attack and passed away, leaving Giselle with both his assets and his debts. The letter she received offered a glimmer of hope for her future.

Claude Abrams resided in sunny Miami, Florida, and he was the great-grandson of Grace Winslow, who worked as a legal stenographer for Strife and Strife Attorneys at Law. It was through this law firm that Bernard crossed paths with Grace, her blonde hair, radiant smile, and graceful figure immediately capturing his attention. They enjoyed a romantic relationship for over a year, but it came to an abrupt end when Grace revealed her pregnancy, and Bernard vanished from her life. Grace, left to fend for herself, gave birth to a son named Alan, who, in turn, raised Louise. Louise eventually married George Abrams, Claude's father.

Claude Abrams was a beachcomber, residing in Miami without any clear source of income. He lived in a modest one-room boat house located in a marina by the ocean. His livelihood included various odd jobs, such as helping unload small fishing boats, closing duties at local restaurants, and even making deliveries for a lumber yard. In his free time, Claude cherished the beach, where he relished the sea, sun, and the simple pleasures of life.

Upon receiving the letter, Claude set it aside, only opening it a week before his scheduled trip to Newport.

⁜ ⁜ ⁜

Bernard was astonishingly selfish, documenting each of his affairs with meticulous detail. He regarded the women in his life as if they were trophies, assigning names to them and providing explicit descriptions of their encounters. Although he kept a watchful eye on all of them, he made no effort to contribute to the upbringing of his children. The act of revisiting his liaisons and indulging in fantasies about his conquests was a source of excitement and satisfaction for him.

However, the consequences of his reckless lifestyle finally caught up with him. At the age of 45, Bernard succumbed to a heart attack while in the company of a prostitute named Francine Dubuque in New Orleans.

Ironically, his sole surviving heirs turned out to be his five illegitimate great-grandchildren, individuals he had never acknowledged or supported during his lifetime.

Chapter Two

Franklin Ginsberg, the attorney representing the Estate of Sir Andrew Van Cleese, dedicated weeks to an exhaustive search for any potential living relatives of the deceased. His mission was to inform them about the upcoming reading of the Last Will And Testament, which required their presence at the Newport Mansion as guests for three nights, from September 5th to the 8th. The estate generously covered all expenses, including airline tickets, which were sent prior to departure, along with cars awaiting their arrival at the airport.

Lester and Simone happened to be on the same flight departing from O'Hare Airport. Unacquainted with each other, they encountered one another at the baggage claim area, where a driver was holding signs bearing their names. The initial meeting was a tad awkward, but they exchanged brief introductions and engaged in minimal conversation as they proceeded to the waiting limousine, their luggage stowed in the trunk. They settled into the car, with Lester eventually breaking the silence by asking, "So, are you from Chicago too?" Simone replied, "No, I'm from Columbus. I had to fly from John Glenn to O'Hare, and now I'm here. My name is Simone Geoffrey, and you are?" Lester introduced himself, saying, "Coonz, Lester Coonz. I'm from Chicago." Simone responded with a warm smile, and they remained quiet for the remainder of the journey.

About an hour later, Giselle Tweed landed, and her driver met her at the baggage claim area, directing her to the waiting limousine. Claude Abrams and Trey Wilson arrived separately, roughly 30 minutes apart, all en route to the Newport Mansion.

Newport was the Mecca of the ultra-wealthy, where decadent mansions and estates flaunted exorbitant prosperity in a competitive display of profligacy. The summer homes here were so lavish and opulent that their sheer preposterousness seemed to insult those who struggled for a humble life.

As Simone peered out of the limousine window, she couldn't help but admire the beauty of Newport. The quaint homes and marina at the town's center passed by her view. Then they drove along tree-lined streets, where 10-foot walls shielded massive structures, hidden from sight except for ornate giant gates, and there was not a soul to be seen walking the streets. "Quite an area, I'd say. Wish I had a couple of these listings," Lester boasted. Simone, intrigued, inquired, "Are you a Realtor?" "Yes, back in Chicago," Lester replied. The small talk subsided as they approached the front gates. "Well, I guess this is it," Lester exclaimed, resembling a child about to enter an amusement park. Simone offered a smile and wished him, "Good luck, Lester. Hope you get the listing."

In front of them stood a massive fountain adorned with mermaids and dolphins, gracing the entrance of an enormous structure at the end of a long circular cobblestone driveway. The limestone exterior boasted intricate details, with great arched doors adorned by the faces of lions on each side. Simone couldn't help but be awestruck by its splendor, while Lester's eyes seemed to see nothing but dollar signs.

Eric Klaus, the Estate Manager, warmly greeted them. He was a humble man, nearly 70 years old, who had spent 52 years in the service of Sir Andrew. His journey had begun when he was just 18, working as a kitchen helper and steadily ascending the ranks through loyalty and dedication. Eric had a deep appreciation for life, having come from a poor German immigrant family. He understood the value of respect and had experienced the pangs of hunger. Now, in his later years and mourning the loss of his employer, Sir Andrew meant much more to him than just a boss. Sir Andrew had been his idol, mentor, and friend.

Eric had essentially grown up in this world – this house, this environment – guided by strict rules and a commitment to fairness. Sir Andrew had taken a liking to Eric, often praising his work, which had led to his current esteemed position. He had his own suite in the servants' section, a space that was much more elaborate and comfortable compared to the quarters of the others who resided there.

Giselle Tweed arrived soon after, followed by Claude Abrams and Trey Wilson. Eric welcomed them in front of the enormous entry doors as they emerged from their limos. They all exchanged brief greetings, acknowledging each other without a formal introduction. Eric stated, "Sir Andrew welcomes you all to his humble home in this time of mourning his passing. I am Eric Klaus, the estate manager. You each are assigned a team to assist in a comfortable stay. Your suites are ready, and your butlers will bring the bags to your rooms. So, if you follow me, I will introduce you. I will be available if you require anything your team cannot provide."

Entering the central vestibule with its 50 ft ceiling, a domed stained glass skylight illuminated the space with sunlight. Five groups of three house staff stood at attention. Each group had two handmaidens and a butler. Eric made the introductions.

"Ms. Tweed, David is your butler, and Anna and Marie will assist him." Each bowed or curtsied as their names were called.

"Mr. Abrams, your butler is Thomas, and Aubrey and Carmen will assist him. Mr. Wilson, your butler is Joseph, and he will be assisted by Linda and Grace. Ms. Geoffrey, your butler is William, and Alice and Fran will assist him. Mr. Coonz, your butler is Philip, and Carol and Nancy will assist. They will guide you from here. Dinner is at 6:30 in the dining room. I hope you find your accommodations acceptable."

With a short bow, he turned and left. Each team exchanged pleasantries with their assigned guests and escorted them up the curved marble staircase to the second level and the bedroom suites.

* * *

Chapter Three

The bedroom suites were grand, with canopy beds opposite massive fireplaces. Each was different and lavishly decorated in harmony with the room's decor. There were soft armchairs, a chaise lounge, and French doors leading out to a balcony overlooking the nearby sea. Each room had a private bath, large and spacious with marble floors, cast porcelain fixtures, a tub, a sink, and a water closet.

After settling the guests and ensuring their comfort, the teams left. Moments later, they were all startled by a shrill scream echoing from the vestibule. Rushing out to the hall to see what had occurred, they looked down from over the Baroque railing surrounding the lower area. Giselle Tweed lay twisted and broken at the bottom of the marble staircase, with a pool of blood swelling from behind her head. There were squeals of shock from the females as the house staff emerged from every direction surrounding Ms. Tweed's body.

Eric reached down to check for a pulse and sorrowfully announced, "She's Gone." Everyone was chattering away at the same time. Eric clapped his hands together, saying, "We must remain calm. It is an unfortunate occurrence. I'll call the Police. May I ask that you all return to your quarters until we look into what happened to Ms. Tweed?"

Simone and Claude were standing next to one another at the rail. Claude half smiled, saying,

"I'm Claude Abrams, and you are?"

"I'm Simone Geoffrey from Ohio."

"Very sad. I wonder how she fell," Claude said, rubbing his chin.

"Why do you say it like that?" Simone replied.

"I don't know. It just seems a little strange to me. A poor woman came here seeking a dream come true."

"Are you looking for your dream come true, Claude?" He stopped and looked into her eyes as his expression changed from sadness to delight. It was like he had seen a vision. "You might think this is crazy, but meeting you is more than I had anticipated. I do hope we can spend more time together." His eyes were warm and inviting, his smile tender and believable.

"Well, it is a pleasure to meet you, too. I wish it were under different circumstances. I'll see you later, Claude." Simone opened the door to her suite.

"Yes, see you later." he said, his eyes never leaving hers.

Eric called the Newport Police, explaining the accident to Desk Sergeant Syms. "I'll pass you to Detective Sam Blanco, Sir. Please hold."

"Detective Blanco, can I help you?"

"There has been a terrible accident at the Van Cleese residence. A woman has fallen down the staircase and is dead. I am Eric Klaus, the housekeeping Manager."

"Mr. Klaus, when did this occur?"

"Just moments ago, Sir."

"I'm on my way. Please do not touch anything, Mr. Klaus."

Sam Blanco was an NYC Detective serving 20 years on the streets of the Big Apple, seeing it all and more. After retiring, Sam and his wife Christina moved to Newport. He joined the Newport Police, looking for a less hectic way of Police work.

Blanco arrived at the Mansion as Eric awaited him at the front doors. Exiting the shiny Black Mercury, he walked towards Eric. His stocky structure was intimidating. Eric said, "Detective Blanco? I'm Eric Klaus this way, Sir."

The sheer size of the vestibule took aback Blanco. He had never been inside one of the many mansions in the area before. He went right to the body, examining it. At that moment, the paramedics and Coroner arrived.

"Mr. Klaus, what did you say happened here?"

"It appears to me that she had fallen down the stairs, Sir."

Blanco looked at the stairs as he walked up. "These steps are pretty wide and deep. Could she have miss-stepped or something? I don't see any tripping hazards. The handrail is certainly wide enough for support. Did anyone see the fall?"

"I don't think so, Detective." Eric seemed nervous.

Two more officers and a forensics specialist arrived. "Where are all the others?"

"The housekeepers and Butlers are all in the kitchen, and the guests are in the suites upstairs."

"I'll need to speak to all of them individually."

"Of Course, Sir."

Blanco went to the officers and said, "Go into the kitchen and get statements from the staff. See if anyone saw or heard anything. I'll speak to the guests. Oh, I need photos of everything."

Blanco slowly walked up the stairs, scanning each step. "Did she fall? Or did someone push her?" He thought, knowing that Sir Andrew had passed, and his will would be settled. He knocked on the first door, and Lester Coonz answered. "I'm Detective Sam Blanco. I'm investigating the death here today of Giselle Tweed. May I have your full name, Sir?"

"Lester Coonz."

"What is your relation to the deceased?"

"I have never met her. We are all here for the reading of the will of our Great Uncle, Sir Andrew Van Cleese. Too bad for her, we're anticipating a substantial award." His eyes were wide with excitement.

"Did you have any conversation with Ms. Tweed?"

"No, I did not."

"Have you left the room at all before the accident?"

"No, been here the entire time. Pretty classy, right? Guess that's more for the rest of us now." Lester showed no sympathy or remorse for Ms Tweed.

"What do you do for a living, Mr. Coonz?"

"Real Estate in Chicago. This inheritance can change my life." His enthusiasm was more than apparent.

Blanco said, "I may need to speak with you again. Mr. Coonz."

"I'll be here for three nights, Detective."

"We'll see, Mr. Coonz. We'll see," as he turned and left the room.

Just as Blanco was about to knock on the next door, Trey Wilson opened it, holding it open for Linda, the Chamber Maid, to exit. "Thank you, Linda." Said Trey with a coy smile.

"Oh, you are very welcome, Sir," she said with a look of embarrassment as she wiped her chin. Blanco backed away as she passed.

"Can I help you, Sir?"

"Sam Blanco, Detective Newport Police." Sam was curt.

"Excuse me, Detective; I didn't realize."

"Can I ask you some questions about Giselle Tweed?"

"Of course, but I don't know her."

"Have you had any conversation with her today?"

"Maybe a hello to be friendly. Other than that, no, Sir."

"Have you been out of the room before the accident?" Trey's face flushed.

"No, Detective, I have been here the entire time. I didn't even know that there was an accident. Is Ms Tweed OK?"

"She's dead, Mr. Wilson."

"What! I'm sorry, Detective."

"I may have to speak with you again, Mr Wilson. What is your Chamber Maids name?"

"Linda, Sir."

Blanco left the room. "Two so far, and I don't like either," he thought.

Next was Simone Geoffrey. Knocking on the door and waiting, knocking again, no answer. The third time the door opened, Simone stood in a towel, saying, "Is there another emergency? Who are you?"

"Excuse me, Mam; I'm Detective Sam Blanco, Newport Police." Trying not to look at her, "I'm sorry to disturb you. May I ask you some questions about Giselle Tweed?"

"Surely, Detective. Would you mind waiting until I get dressed?"

"My apologies, Mam. I'll come back."

"Thank you." With that, Simone closed the door.

Blanco went to the next door and knocked. No answer. He Knocked again and waited with no response. Philip the Butler was walking down the hall and said, "That is Ms. Tweeds' room, Sir."

Blanco looked over at him, asking. "Is it open?"

"I'll open it for you, Sir." And he did.

"Thank you, and you are?"

"Philip, Sir, I'm assisting Mr. Coonz with his stay—such a trag-edy today, that poor woman. I guess you never know. So sad."

"Yes, you never know. Do you know if Mr. Coonz left his room today?"

"Don't know, Sir."

Blanco entered the room, leaving the door open. Alone now, he looked around and was amazed at the luxurious abode and the comfort level of the furnishings. "Christina would love this," he said out loud.

Anna put Ms. Tweed's things away in an elaborate French pro-vincial piece. He briefly looked through her things but found noth-ing of interest. He opened the drawer on a bedside table, and her purse was inside. Opening it was some papers. One of the letters was inviting her to the reading of the will. The other from her bank advised her that due to a substantial amount of payments in ar-rears, the bank was to foreclose on her apartment. Blanco put it back. "Guess you never know," he thought. There was nothing else, so he went back next door.

Simone Geoffrey opened. She was stunning, dressed in a black dress, very tight, accentuating her curves. It was short, exposing her muscular calves and high-heeled open shoes. Her hair was up, her green eyes sparkling. Her smile was radiant.

"Well, Detective. What can I help you with?" She said with confidence.

"Did you leave the room at all today? Ms. Geoffrey."

"No, only when I heard the scream. I ran out to see everyone surrounding that unfortunate woman."

"Did you know Ms. Tweed?"

"No, I don't know any of the guests."

"Did you have any conversation with Ms. Tweed? Or anyone else?"

"I didn't speak to Ms. Tweed. I rode from the airport with Lester Coonz. He's an odd one."

"What do you mean, Odd?"

"He seemed very excited about the inheritance. We all are, I guess. But he was almost in a euphoric state about it. His eyes were a little creepy to me. I also spoke with Claude Abrams. He's nice."

"What did you say to Mr. Abrams?"

"Not much, just introductions, we responded to the scream. Seeing that woman at the bottom of the stairs." Simone almost whimpered, but she caught herself. "Thank you, Ms. Geoffrey. I may come back to you."

Next, Claude Abrams. Blanco knocked, and the door opened, and a man was standing there, bare-chested, bare feet, in flower-covered Hawaiian shorts, holding a fruit drink in his hand.

"Can I help you?"

"Detective Sam Blanco, I'm investigating the Death of Ms. Tweed. Can you tell me if you left your room today?"

"Only after hearing the scream."

"Did you have any conversations with anyone?"

"Only Simone Geoffrey. We met at the rail, looking down at that distressing sight. It isn't pleasant. What do you think happened, Detective? Did she fall? Or was she pushed?"

"Pushed? What makes you think that she was pushed? Mr. Abrams."

"I don't know, Detective. I have a gut feeling that it wasn't a fall. I saw Giselle when she arrived. I didn't speak to her, but my assessment of her wasn't that she was frail. She seemed strong and elegantly dressed. She certainly, in my opinion, took care of herself."

"Thank you, Mr. Abrams; I'll get back to you." And he left the room.

Chapter Four

Blanco called the precinct and asked Sergeant Syms, "I need everything you can find on Giselle Tweed, Lester Coonz, Trey Wilson, Claude Abrams, and Simone Geoffrey. ASAP OK? Thanks, Seargent." Then he called Christina.

"Hi, Sweetheart. You will never guess where I am."

"Oh, Hi, Sam. Where?"

"I'm at one of the mansions. You have got to see this. It's like a Fairy Tale Palace. Listen, I'm going to be here awhile. I'm sorry, Honey."

"No worries, Sam. I love you. Be careful."

"Love you too, Sweetheart."

Sam went into the kitchen, where the officers took the statements he requested.

"Where is Eric Klaus?"

"He would be in his quarters, Sir." One of the butlers responded and directed him to the door.

Eric answered quickly, opening. "Detective, what is it that I can assist you with?"

"Mr. Klaus, how long have you been employed at the estate?"

"52 years, Sir, This February."

"That's quite a long time, Sir."

"Yes! Glorious years, Sir."

"How was your relationship with Sir Andrew?"

"He was a great man, Sir. Kind, generous, fair. He was my mentor, teaching me many things about life and the world. I want to think of him as my friend. His loss is heartbreaking for me and the Staff."

"Was anyone assigned to the second floor before Ms.Tweed fell?"

"Yes, of course, every guest had three aids, and they were settling in when this terrible thing happened to Ms.Tweed."

"Where were you when she fell?"

"I, I, Well, I was in the kitchen working with the Chef for dinner tonight. You don't think I had anything to do with her death?"

"What's the Chef's name?"

"Pierre."

"Thank you, Eric."

Blanco went out to the vestibule as the Coroner was removing the body. "Dr. Rojas. What do you think?" Blanco asked.

"Well, without further analysis, she has a broken neck, but she has a strange wound on the back of her head not conducive to the fall."

"What are you saying, Doctor?"

"She may have been struck with something."

"Thank you, Sir; please let me know as soon as possible."

"Yes, Surely, Detective."

The dining room was set for four guests at the massive mahogany table; up to 18 people could be served. The high-backed chairs were carved with precision craftsmanship, with center backs cushioned and soft velvet seats. Three gigantic candelabras were spaced accordingly on the table, flamboyantly wallpapered in gold leaf, Baroque moldings, and a fireplace graciously Gold in color. Butlers and handmaidens stood ready to serve their every wish.

At 6:30, the guests arrived and exchanged introductions. They were all properly dressed in formal attire and were seated as Eric came in. "Good evening. Our Chef Pierre has prepared a wonderful meal for you all this evening. I hope you enjoy it, and anything you desire; please don't hesitate to ask one of our Staff." With that, the handmaidens began serving the soup. Simone asked, "What do you think about this woeful accident today?" The others fidgeted in their seats as Claude said, "I don't think it was an accident."

"What are you saying?" said Lester. "The woman tripped over her own feet. Maybe she was drunk or something."

"That's an assumption by both of you. We have to wait for the report," Trey said. "This soup is sublime," Lester touted. "I guess that means more for us? Right? Now that she is gone. Four, not five?"

"What an awful callous thing to say," Simone was angry.

Detective Blanco came into the room. "Excuse me, sorry to interrupt your meal, but I just wanted you to know the coroner's report shows that Ms. Tweed was murdered." Everyone responded with surprise except Claude. "There, I told you it wasn't an accident."

Blanco continued, "That makes everyone in the house a suspect. You all must remain here as the investigation continues." Lester yelled out, "What about the will? I want my inheritance!"

"Shut up, Lester!" Trey said. "What's the matter with you? A poor woman has lost her life, and you are worried about money?"

"I'm just saying that it shouldn't hold anything up." The second course came out: Roasted Quayle with tomatoes, onions, and carrots. Blanco said, "Enjoy your meal, folks. I'll be around."

Claude was trying to make eye contact with Simone, who was not responding. Trey passed a note to Linda, the handmaiden, as she took away the soup dishes. The meal continued in silence. Lester finished, took his napkin, dropped it on his plate, and left the room.

Simone sat back, sipping her coffee, assessing the room. Trey said, "If you will excuse me, I'm going to my room." Claude stood beside Simone, saying, "Mind if I sit here?"

"Please sit down," she responded with a smile. "So we are all suspects. I guess that leaves me out. I didn't do it. Did you?" He said with a smile and in jest. Simone's face got solemn; looking directly into his eyes, she said. "You never know. You never know."

Jaw dropped, and Simone laughed. "Got Cha!" Claude sat back and sighed. "You shocked the breath out of me." "Well, it was easy enough."

Simone was lovely, prim, and proper, but with an unusual heir about her—a mysterious, foxy, and alluring manner. Claude liked her. "I have to go to my room, so I guess I'll see you tomorrow." Claude was disappointed, and he wanted to get to know her a little better. "I'll walk with you to your room." "OK." They walked as Claude tried connecting with her, with little success. At her door, she just said, "Good night, Claude. See you tomorrow." He went to his room, feeling rejected.

Trey entered the library and closed the door. Waiting in the corner was Linda, the chambermaid. She was seductive and alluring. Her blonde hair was up in a bun with her maid cap. Her dark eyes sensually looked across the room at him. Her smile enticed him as she parted her lips bewitchingly. Trey's heart pounded with anticipation. She was tall and voluptuous standing there. Her legs were long and perfectly shaped, inviting him. He walked to her as his excitement grew.

With the most enchanting voice, she said "May I help you, sir?" She unbuttoned the front of her house dress, exposing the cleavage of her large, firm breasts. He took her into his arms breathlessly, saying, "Linda."

They embraced with a kiss so passionately that they almost stumbled. Linda moved him to the couch, kissing his neck while undoing his shirt. Kissing and lightly licking his chest and stomach as she opened his pants. Trey was in ecstasy as Linda enticed him with her oral skills. She captivated him with pleasure. Pulling her up to him, he kissed her and turned her around, undressing her. She pulled away and sat him down to watch her tease him while removing her clothes, dazzling him with her perfect body.

She was exquisite and irresistible. He brought her to him, and he kissed every inch of her. She was entranced by his tenderness, which excited her to climax time after time. She was pushing him back on the chaise lounge and mounting him. Slowly, she moved her hips, rolling like a hula dancer. Trey had been with many women in his day, but Linda was statuesque. He had never experienced such raw intensity from a lover.

As they reached a crescendo, someone struck Linda on the side of her head, knocking her to the floor. Trey jumped up as he was struck in the temple, causing him to fall, crashing atop the coffee table, his arm draped across Linda's limp body. Lovers were obliterated at the height of enthusiasm.

Hours later, screams reverberated throughout the mansion when Mary found the bodies. Again, all the staff ran to her aid. In the library, they discovered Trey and Linda, naked, with Trey's arm draped over Linda in a twisted pose of erotic death. Their blood mingled all over the floor.

Eric announced, "No one touches anything. I'll call Detective Blanco. Now, everyone out!"

Eric went to the phone and called the police. Sergeant Syms answered, "Newport Police, can I help you?"

"This is Eric Klaus. There has been another murder at the Mansion. I need someone here ASAP."

"I'll call Detective Blanco, Sir."

Blanco arrived looking for Eric. "What happened here?"

"In the library, Sir."

Blanco opened the library door as Eric appeared behind him. "No one leaves the mansion." Blanco was in his game now.

"Wait out here," he said and entered the room with its wood-paneled ceiling, each square intricately carved with children playing in gardens, Cherubs primping proper ladies, truly amazing to behold. Comfort abounded with leather couches, soft cushioned chairs, and walls lined with books. The focal point was the imported French fireplace carved in chocolate-colored marble brilliantly polished, making it shine like a gemstone. The windows were covered floor to ceiling with tapestries, a perfect hiding place. He looked behind each, finding nothing. He stood over the bodies and thought, "They never saw it coming. Total surprise. It could be anyone."

Eric went back to the kitchen and called a meeting. "Detective Blanco said we are all suspects in these gruesome attacks. No one is to leave the Mansion. Are there any questions?"

"Who could do such things? Why?" asked Carol, Lester's hand-maiden, whimpering.

"I don't know, and I pray it's not any of you," said Eric. They all started mumbling in offense.

"OK, there is work to be done. Let's have at it," he said sharply, clapping his hands. They all started slowly to leave, huddling in small groups. "Let's go! Let's go!" he coaxed them.

Chapter Five

Blanco combed the room when the Coroner arrived with the forensic team. After examining the bodies, Dr. Rojas said, "The wounds to the head look similar to Ms. Tweed's. I'll make a further analysis at the morgue."

"Thank you, Doc," said Blanco as he went out of the room to brief the Patrolmen to "Keep everything secure and no one leaves.

Back in the Library, he looked at everything. The colossal marble fireplace interested him, remembering that secret passages could be possible in old mansions like this. So he ran his fingers along the inner edges of the fire chamber and noticed some scratches on the wood floor surface. His curiosity stirred.

A candle holder was on the wall above the marks; he touched it at the bottom, pushed an almost undetectable button, and opened it like a magic door. His adrenaline surged as he entered a small chamber with a staircase leading down. Flicking on his flashlight and holding his .32 snub nose, he descended the stone stairs while his heart throbbed. At the bottom, the room opened to what resembled a theater with rows of seats like pews facing an altar and podium. Turning with his light, he saw entries to this alcove around its circular space. Each had an opening to long dark tunnels.

He approached the altar, its surface covered with a black silk table linen, embroidered with a large modified gold infinity monogram surrounded by stars and above it all stitched in old English lettering the word DOMINATA. The back altar had carvings of nude men and women climbing up a rock-covered surface, all reaching up as if trying to escape the depths below. In the center, there was a gold door. It was locked as Blanco, in his suspicion, wanted to open it.

"What is this place?" His thoughts raced as he turned to the podium and, on its top, a voluminous book. Its cover was elaborately designed and inscribed DOMINATA. He needed help down here, so he returned to the upper floor of the Mansion.

Blanco needed some rest. It was already 2 in the morning, and the forensic team was busy working, with patrolmen posted. So he went home to Christina.

He pulled into the attached garage of the small cape-style house. In the mudroom, he removed his shoes and hung his jacket. The house had two bedrooms, a nice kitchen, a living room, and a dining room combination. One of the bedrooms was small and had a bathroom, while the primary bedroom was larger and had a full bathroom with a walk-in shower.

Quietly as he could, he undressed and showered. Then, he slipped into bed next to his beautiful wife, Christina. Trying not to wake her, he positioned himself with his back to her and attempted to sleep. However, moments later, he felt the heat of her naked body against him, her arm around him, touching him as she kissed the back of his neck.

"Welcome home, Detective Blanco," she said in the sexiest, raspy voice. Christina was his dream come true—sweet, loving, devoted, funny, a great cook, and gorgeous. The passion quickly ignited between them as they embraced, exchanging intimate acts of tenderness and ecstasy. He adored her. He had never truly known love until Christina was in his life. She loved Sam deeply, catering to his every need, wish, and desire.

• • •

They lived happily in their little love nest.

After reaching an explosive climax, they lay there holding each other, and she said, "So, how was your day?" He chuckled. "I love you, Christina." And they slept.

The kitchen was prepping for the daily meals for the three remaining guests when Eric was alerted that the attorney retained to read the will had arrived. Franklin Ginsberg was a 75-year-old attorney who had worked with Sir Andrew for decades. He was short, balding, his circular wire-rimmed glasses resting at the end of his nose. His three-piece suit seemed ill-fitting, as the jacket appeared too large for his frail frame. He walked with a cane adorned with a silver dragon head handle. Eric greeted him as he disembarked from the limo.

"Good morning, Mr. Ginsberg. Please allow Peter to assist you with your things. You are just in time for breakfast. The staff will be serving shortly. Would you like to clean up from your trip? Peter, please escort Mr. Ginsberg to his suite." Ginsberg simply nodded and followed Peter into the mansion.

Simone emerged from her chambers and descended the stairs as Claude said, "Good morning, Simone." He waved and smiled as he hurried to catch up to her. She returned the smile and replied, "Good morning, Claude. How was your night after all that had happened? I'm distraught over this."

"I'm upset too. We are all in danger. We should all stay together as much as possible," Claude responded. Simone looked into his eyes and confessed, "I'm scared, Claude." He took her hands in his and reassured her, "I won't let anything happen to you, Simone." She suddenly began to appreciate this man. He seemed trustworthy and honest. He might not have been her type in terms of appearance, but he had his own attractiveness and made her feel better.

They entered the dining room, where Lester was already indulging himself with scones and fruit. Simone greeted him, saying, "Good morning, Lester." He looked up between bites, waved his hand while holding a slice of pineapple, and replied with a muffled response.

* * *

The staff was quick to attend to them, pouring coffee as they inquired about their chosen entrees. As they looked towards the door, Franklin Ginsberg appeared, strolling to the head of the table without uttering a word. He stood in front of his chair and introduced himself, saying, "I am Franklin Ginsberg. I'm the attorney representing Sir Andrew Van Cleese. I understand there have been some unsavory events here yesterday. I hope that the rest of our stay is pleasant and safe." He then sat down, and Grace hurried to his side.

Claude and Simone greeted him with a "Good morning," while Lester made a gesture of a wave. During the meal, Lester, in all his inappropriateness, blurted out, "So, Mr. Ginsberg! Now that only 3 of us are left, do we get a bigger share, right?" The attorney slowly removed his glasses, taking a cloth to clean the lenses, and looked at Lester with scorn. "What makes you think there is anything to share, sir?" Lester sat back in his chair, puzzled. He finished his meal quietly, then dropped his napkin on his plate and left the room without a word. Simone and Claude also finished their meals, cordially wished Mr. Ginsberg a good day, and left the room.

Chapter Six

Thomas the Butler was on the second floor, checking the suites, as he had done daily for the ten years he served Sir Andrew. His task was to ensure they were dust-free and clean, ready for any unexpected guests.

He entered the Blue Room, one of the suites named after its decor, and meticulously inspected everything with a white glove. As he reached the fireplace, he noticed that one of the side panels was open. Confused, he thought to himself, "What is this?" He had never encountered any hidden doors before. Curiosity got the better of him, and he decided to pull the panel open. However, as he grabbed the edge, a hard object struck him severely on the side of his head, causing him to collapse to the floor like a deflated balloon.

Meanwhile, back in the kitchen, Eric, the head of the staff, addressed the team. "We need to prepare the Study for tomorrow's reading of the will. It must be immaculate. So let's get to work!" He clapped his hands, and he too began inspecting the main floor.

Handmaidens were busy dusting and polishing floors, while a crew entered the Study. The Study was another grand room, with a magnificent hand-carved desk and chair placed in front of a wooden-trimmed fireplace. The intricate carvings on the furniture were a sight to behold. When the draperies were opened, the room was bathed in a warm glow. Every piece of furniture and wall was beautifully handcrafted. Three cushioned chairs were arranged facing the heavy desk, each accompanied by a side table with a pen and a pad. Eric returned after about an hour to ensure that everything met his high standards.

Suddenly, a scream echoed from the second floor. Everyone rushed to see what had happened, including two responding police officers who entered the Blue Room. There, they found Thomas's lifeless body lying in a crumpled heap next to the fireplace. Carmen, the chambermaid, had discovered him and was now standing at the door, crying and trembling with fear.

Blanco was in his office trying to piece things together. The Coroner confirmed it was the same weapon and that the assailant was possibly left-handed. "That should narrow my suspect list," he thought. "Who would benefit from these deaths? Who is left? The heirs, Eric, and the Staff. Pretty much all of them." He paced back and forth.

"The passageways! Where do they lead?" He got on the phone. "Sergeant, l need six men ASAP." "Yes, Sir." Then Patrolman Phelps called in about Thomas' Death. "I'm on my way!" He said, "What's happening there?" He reached the Mansion with the officers. "l need to check this first; take statements from the entire Staff. There's been another murder. Everyone is a suspect. Take note of any southpaws." He ran inside. The cops at the Mansion did a great job of containing the group. "Where did it happen?" He asked Patrolman Phelps. "Upstairs, Detective." Blanco ran up the long staircase.

Eric was there with a Patrolman at the door.

"Where are the Heirs?" Blanco inquired.

"l believe they are all in their rooms, Sir," the Patrolman replied.

Blanco entered the room. There was nothing out of order; the place was pristine. He approached the body, carefully examining the severe head wound. "Who could do this?" he muttered to himself. "What did Thomas do? What did he find? What did he see?" His eyes darted around the fireplace, searching for levers or buttons, but found none. Confused and frustrated, Blanco left the room.

"Let the forensic team go over it," he directed. "You two, go to each guest and take a statement. I want to know anything related to this and if they are left-handed. Got it?"

"Yes, Sir, right on it, Sir," the officers acknowledged before setting off to gather statements.

Blanco went downstairs and gathered his six men. Together, they made their way to the Library. As they approached the fireplace, Blanco pushed the button on the candlestick, causing the secret door to swing open, much to the astonishment of the six Patrolmen.

"Come on! Let's get this done," Blanco urged, switching on his flashlight. He led them down into the main chamber and continued, "Okay, split into pairs and explore these tunnels. Find out where they lead. Take this chalk and mark the way. Be careful. Let's solve this case."

"Yes, Sir!" they responded in unison as they ventured into their assigned tunnels.

Blanco then made his way to the altar and stood at the podium. He stopped, looking down at the book, and read its title aloud, "DOMINATA." With a sense of urgency, he picked up the heavy volume and hurried upstairs to find Eric.

"Do you know anything about the secret passages in this house?" Blanco inquired. Eric appeared uneasy, his gaze fixated on the book.

"Well, do you?" Blanco pressed.

"Yes, Detective, they haven't been used in years," Eric admitted reluctantly.

"What are they for?"

"Years ago, they were a means of escape in an emergency."

"Where do the tunnels go?"

"Tunnels? Sir, I know nothing of tunnels, Sir. Have you ever been through the passages?"

"All I know, Sir, is that they connect all the rooms."

"Where were you when Thomas was murdered?"

"Sir? I was with the Staff. Surely you don't think I had anything to do with this."

"What do you know about DOMINATA?" Blanco's tone grew more insistent.

Eric, now agitated, replied, "I know nothing, Sir. Nothing."

Blanco then said, "May I look through your quarters?"

"I beg your pardon, Sir, is it essential for that?"

"Okay, Mr. Klaus. We'll speak again."

Blanco put the book in his car and then returned to the tunnels. Officers Doug Lewis and Todd French were stationed in front of one of the tunnels when Blanco approached.

"What did you find so far?" Blanco inquired.

"Well, Sir, two tunnels branch off and go upstairs to suites, but their ends were bricked up," Officer Lewis reported.

"What do you mean bricked up?" Blanco sought clarification.

"They were long, deep tunnels, Sir, and then just closed off," Officer French explained.

"Thanks, guys, you've done a great job. Are there any left to cover?" Blanco asked.

"Yes, Sir, we'll keep at it," they replied.

● ● ●

Shortly after, Officers Troy Lake and Fred Chism arrived, followed by Steve Wilson and Jacob Cox. Blanco inquired about their progress.

"How did it go, guys?" he asked.

"Fine, Sir," Jacob replied. "We went into three tunnels, two splits, one going up to the house and the others to a dead end. But the third one continued pretty far. We marked it where we stopped to come back to. That one needs some time to investigate."

Officer Lake shared a similar report, saying, "Sir, we did the same thing, but we had two long ones. We marked them, Sir."

"Okay, keep at it, guys. I'll get you more help," Blanco instructed.

Blanco then returned upstairs to the Library and took a seat at a desk to ponder the situation.

"Eric is my main suspect. He has the most to lose here if the Mansion is sold. Where would he go? Then there is Lester Coons—crude, rude, money-hungry, and anxious. But would he be able to kill? Simone Geoffrey. Not likely; she shows no signs of greed. Claude Abrams. I can't figure him out yet. He seems okay, but you never know. The Staff—could they all be involved in this? No. The tunnels, what's up with them? And DOMINATA? I have to look at that book."

The Coroner's team transported Thomas' body to the morgue, and lunch was served promptly at 1 pm. The four guests made their way to the dining room, with Simone and Claude entering together and greeting the others with a simple "Good Afternoon." Lester, on the other hand, wasted no time and took his seat immediately. Mr. Ginsberg acknowledged the greeting, but the atmosphere was tense, and conversation was notably absent.

Blanco entered the dining room, his presence commanding attention. "Good Afternoon; we have had four killings in 2 days here. You know you are all suspects except for Mr. Ginsberg, who has just arrived," he declared sternly. "I realize you live away from here and are all present on serious business, but I have to ask you not to leave until we have reached some conclusions."

Silence hung in the air, broken only by Lester's defiant outburst. "You can't keep us here. I want what's coming to me, and I'm gone!"

Blanco addressed him firmly, "Mr. Coonz, remember you are detained as a prime suspect in a murder investigation. I hope that you all will continue to cooperate. Mr. Coonz, you can enjoy the comforts of our jail if you choose."

With that, Blanco left the room, leaving the guests to contemplate the gravity of the situation.

Chapter Seven

Philip the Butler and Nancy the Chambermaid were in love, and they carried on their passion for almost 18 months while employed by Sir Andrew. No one knew or even suspected their romance. They would meet in different suites every few days to indulge in passionate liaisons.

Their Affaires de Coer were creative and discreet.

Philip was tall lean, with chiseled features. His eyes were green, and his hair blonde cut short and proper, his smile hypnotizing to Nancy, who also was tall and sleek, with long slender legs hidden under her maid dress. Her body was a sculptured masterpiece for Philip's eyes only. Her eyes were blue, her skin was like a porcelain doll, and her dark hair was thick and curly.

They met in the green room just after lunch. Philip entered as Nancy was already there. She stood in the bathroom doorway; she was nude, her skin glistening from the oils she had applied. Philip locked the door behind him and slowly walked to her, admiring her loveliness. His heart began racing as his eagerness intensified. "You are so beautiful. My Love." He said as his arousal grew.

He stopped in front of her and lightly, with his fingertips, caressed her shoulders, arms, face, and neck as he gently kissed her plump red lips. Their fervor escalated as she began removing his clothing. He picked her up as they kissed and carried her to the canopy bed, laying her softly on the mattress. Taking her ankle in his hand, he kissed her toes, then delicately licked his way up her leg as his fingers caressed her firm, shapely breasts. Reaching her femininity, he used his tongue and lips to explore her most intimate regions. She quivered with delight. His excitement peaked as he mounted her, penetrating her slowly as she squealed softly in jubilation. His pace increased and slowed, repeatedly, bringing her to heights of delirium until him, too, reached raptures of intoxication.

They reached the pinnacle of their passion, experiencing an eruption of fulfillment. Lying spent in each other's arms, they basked in the afterglow. Suddenly, the side panel of the fireplace slid open, breaking the tranquility of the moment. Nancy, still in a daze, awoke to the sight of a dark shadow looming over her. Before she could react, the head of a mallet came crashing down on her head, shattering the peaceful scene. Philip, startled by the commotion, awakened just in time to witness the brutal blow that met him. Love and death intertwined as a scarlet pool expanded on the once pristine sheets.

In another location, Sergeant Syms placed a call to Blanco at the mansion. Joseph, the Butler, found Blanco in the Study and informed him of the call. Blanco picked up the phone on the desk, his voice steady. "Detective Blanco, can I help you?" he inquired.

"Sergeant Syms here, Sir. I have the background checks you requested. All are clean except for Giselle Tweed. It appears she has a history of priors on her rap sheet. Disorderly conduct, public intoxication with violence, and she's currently on parole, attending AA meetings," Sergeant Syms reported.

"Thanks, Sergeant. Good work," Blanco acknowledged, leaning back in his chair. Contemplating the new information, he wondered, "Could she have been intoxicated and had a drunken fall?"

Blanco decided to reach out to Dr. Rojas at the morgue for further insights. He dialed the number and was greeted by Alison Chambers, who answered the call. "City Morgue, Alison Chambers speaking."

"This is Detective Sam Blanco. Is Dr. Rojas available?" Blanco inquired.

"He's here, Sir. Let me see if he can come to the phone," Alison responded, putting Blanco on hold briefly. After a short pause, Dr. Rojas's voice came through the line. "Dr. Rojas speaking. How are you, Sam? How can I help you?"

Blanco got straight to the point. "Well, Doc, is there a chance that you can perform a toxicology report on Giselle Tweed? Could she have been intoxicated when she fell?"

Dr. Rojas considered Blanco's request. "If I recall correctly, her liver did show signs of cirrhosis. Let me delve deeper into the records. Is there a specific concern?"

"I want to ensure that her fall wasn't related to intoxication. She had a known history of substance abuse," Blanco explained, hoping to uncover more details.

"I'll look into it and get back to you, Sam," Dr. Rojas assured him.

As Blanco hung up the phone, he couldn't help but think, "This could change everything." The possibility that Giselle's death might be linked to her struggles with alcoholism opened up a new avenue of investigation.

Simone and Claude were spending more time together as they strolled the property and the gardens, talking, laughing, and getting to trust one another. Claude was funny and entertaining, more intelligent than he tended to portray. Simone was beginning to like him. He was fascinated with her. Dinner was approaching, so he walked her to her suite to freshen up, and she said. "Thank you, Claude, for not giving up on me. I don't make acquaintances easily. I like you." And she kissed him on the cheek. Claude's eyes said it all. "My pleasure, my lady." He removed an imaginary hat and bowed before her. She giggled and went inside. Claude was elated.

Lester leisurely strolled through the opulent halls, admiring the lavish decor of each room. Intrigued by a flicker of movement near the fireplace, he approached cautiously, only to find nothing amiss. "What was that?" he wondered, his fingers skimming along the smooth edge of the marble fire chamber. Accidentally, he brushed against a concealed switch, and to his surprise, a panel swung open like a secret doorway. Driven by curiosity, he ventured inside, only for the panel to close behind him, trapping him in the oppressive darkness. The inky blackness enveloped him, rendering him blind. Desperate, he pounded on the walls, his voice echoing through the confined space. "Help! Help me! Help!" he cried out, his pleas reverberating in the eerie silence. Inch by inch, he sidestepped, banging and shouting with all his might. Suddenly, without warning, he reached the edge of a staircase and tumbled down uncontrollably, losing consciousness in the pitch-black abyss.

Meanwhile, in the bustling kitchen, Eric busied himself with preparations for dinner service. Pierre LaMonte, the esteemed chef, meticulously crafted a menu featuring Beef Wellington, accompanied by a medley of baby vegetables and a shrimp cocktail appetizer with cream of mushroom soup. The indulgent finale would be Creme Brûlée with Espresso. The table would be adorned with champagne and refined liqueurs, offering a touch of elegance.

Pierre, a strikingly handsome young man, had been handpicked by Sir Andrew himself after a visit to Paris. The flavors and culinary artistry showcased by Pierre had captivated Sir Andrew, prompting him to bring the talented chef to America three years prior. Pierre's love for cooking was surpassed only by his passion for women. Throughout the day, he effortlessly charmed the female staff, leaving them daydreaming about him. Each woman felt as though she held a special place in Pierre's heart, thanks to his masterful flirtations. He indulged in romantic interludes with many of them, his seductive accent adding to the allure. His dark, mesmerizing eyes cast a spell on the women, captivating their attention. With his suave charm and melodic voice, Pierre made them feel like queens, creating an atmosphere akin to a personal harem, where he could choose whomever he desired, and they willingly embraced their roles.

Chapter Eight

Claude knocked on Simone's door to escort her to dinner. She opened with a smile. "Hi Claude, I'm ready." Claude grinned and playfully twirled her, eliciting laughter from Simone. They entered the dining room, where Mr. Ginsberg had already taken his place at the head of the table. In unison, Simone and Claude greeted him, saying, "Good Evening, Mr. Ginsberg," to which he responded with a nod of acknowledgment. The staff stood ready, patiently waiting for Lester Coonz.

Several minutes passed in silence, and Mr. Ginsberg finally spoke, "It seems Mr. Coonz is not attending this evening. May we proceed?" Simone and Claude nodded in agreement, and the first course was served. They dined quietly until Claude broke the silence, "It's odd that Lester, of all people, is not here." Simone concurred, "Yes, he's usually the first one to arrive." Mr. Ginsberg continued eating, seemingly unfazed by Lester's absence.

Claude called over David, the Butler, and requested, "Could you please go to Mr. Coonz's room to see if he's alright?" David promptly replied, "At once, Sir," and left the room. Simone, Claude, and Mr. Ginsberg finished their dessert while awaiting David's return. When he did, David wore a somber expression, "I'm sorry, Sir, but Mr. Coonz is not in his room."

Meanwhile, Detective Blanco was in need of a break. He headed to the Library with the intention of exploring the tunnels. In the Vestibule, Claude and Simone called out to him, and Blanco approached them. "Is there something I can help you with?" he asked. Simone explained the situation, "Lester Coonz didn't come to dinner, and he's not in his room."

Blanco was concerned, "Not in his room? He has to be in the house. I have officers posted outside." Claude offered a suggestion, "We can have the staff search for him; that might help." Blanco agreed and said, "Let me go find Eric." He headed for the kitchen, where Eric was still overseeing the cleanup. Blanco inquired, "Mr. Klaus, have you seen Mr. Coonz?" Eric replied, "Why, No, Sir, I've been here working." Blanco then made a request, "Can you organize the staff to search for him?" Eric agreed, "Certainly, Detective." He went to a corner of the kitchen, where he pulled a long tapestry with tassels at the bottom, causing a low gong sound to resonate throughout the Mansion.

Within moments, the kitchen was filled with staff members, ready to assist. Blanco commended them, saying, "Impressive." He then explained the situation, "Mr. Coonz is missing. If you could search the house to find him, it would greatly help me." Eric took charge, clapping his hands and issuing orders, "Let's get to it!" The staff members responded, "Yes, Sir!" and quickly dispersed throughout the Mansion. Blanco thanked Mr. Klaus, who replied sarcastically, "At your service, Sir."

Blanco then proceeded to the Library and descended into the tunnels. With the presence of generators, the chambers were well-lit. The search team had expanded, and officers and staff were working together to investigate the chambers.

Blanco was pleased with the progress. Officer French approached Blanco and said, "Detective, we've made great discoveries, Sir. So far, three tunnels lead to other mansions. We are going to need warrants to proceed from there. It looks to me, Sir, that members of this group live in the immediate area and meet here as a hub for whatever they believe in."

• • •

"Nice work, French. How many more are there?" Blanco inquired.

"A guess, Sir, would be over 50."

"What!" Blanco was stunned. "What kind of can of worms did we open here?" "This is big, Detective. Really Big."

Suddenly, an officer emerged from a tunnel, saying, "Detective, we found someone. This way, Sir." Blanco and French followed him into another tunnel, and on the ground, being attended to, was Lester Coonz. He was battered from the fall and a little bruised, but he was okay.

"Mr. Coonz, are you okay?" Blanco asked.

"Yes, Yes, Detective, I'm a bit shaken, but I'll survive."

"So what brings you here, Mr. Coonz?" Blanco inquired.

"I was cruising the rooms, checking out my inheritance, and I found a secret panel by a fireplace. I went in to see what it was and fell down the stairs. It was pretty dark then."

Blanco instructed the officers, "Officers, can you assist Mr. Coonz back upstairs to his suite? Thank you. Oh, Mr. Coonz. No more roaming around. OK?"

"Do you think that I can get something to eat now?" Coonz asked.

Blanco just went upstairs, reflecting on the situation. "This is no cakewalk. To think I retired up here to make it easier. Ha!" He thought.

As he returned to the vestibule, more screams pierced the air. "Oh, My God! Oh! My God!" Alice, the chambermaid, had found the lifeless bodies of Philip and Nancy. Her screams echoed through the Mansion. Blanco ran up the stairs as everyone converged on the Green Room.

"OK! OK! Everybody out!" Blanco took charge. A few officers were there with them, trying to control the crowd. Maids were crying, butlers were revolted, and chaos reigned. Claude comforted Simone, while Eric attempted to assist in calming things down. Mr. Ginsberg, however, walked by without a word and disappeared into his room.

Blanco examined the bodies and the surrounding area. The wounds were similar to the others. He went to the fireplace, skimming his fingers along the edges, and it opened on the left side. He flicked on his flashlight and went in. Following a passage for a time, he shined his light down and saw footprints on the dusty floor. "GOTCHA!" He exclaimed as he backed out of the room.

"OK, keep this room closed until the Coroner gets here with his team. I'll be downstairs," he ordered.

He returned to the Study and called Sergeant Syms. "Sergeant, please get in touch with the Coroner again. I have a double one here for him, and I need forensics with cameras."

"You got it, Detective."

Blanco then called Christina. "Hello!" Her voice instantly made him smile, "Hi, Sweetheart; sorry I haven't called."

"Hi Sam, I miss you, Honey."

"This case has got me concerned. Every time I think I have a break, it changes. I love you and miss you too."

"I know Sam. Just be careful. I'll have something special for you when you come home."

"The best part for me is knowing you are there waiting for me, Sweetheart. I'll call you when I can. Love you."

"I love you, Honey."

He hung up and sat back in his chair. "I have to get something to eat." So he went into the kitchen. Pierre was prepping. "Crazy times around here, eh? Detective," he said with a sharp accent. "How long have you been here, Pierre?"

"Oh, I would say over three years."

"So you know everyone pretty well."

"You might say."

"Who do you think could have done these things?" Blanco asked as he picked up a carrot slice.

"Are you hungry, Detective?" Pierre smiled. "Let me prepare something for you."

"I couldn't accept anything."

"I insist. It would be my pleasure. Please." And he turned and walked to the fridge. "You didn't answer my question. Who do you think could have done these things?"

"Hard to say. Is it Anger? Greed? Maybe both, perhaps maybe Jealousy," he said as he brought out a baked chicken, sliced French bread with butter, and a plate of string beans. "Here, Detective, this was left from the staff dinner. Enjoy." His smile was warm with a hint of deceit.

Blanco ate the savory meal with precision, enjoying every morsel. Eric came in and said, "Making yourself comfortable? Detective."

Pierre said, "I was clearing the staff dinner and offered the Detective some food. My choice, Eric, not his."

"Are you aware of what has occurred?" Pierre had a puzzled look on his face.

Angrily, Eric stated. "Philip and Nancy were murdered."

Pierre dropped a pot of water in surprise. "How can that be? I can't believe it." And in a switch of personality, Pierre said, "How can you sit there eating chicken with my Nancy upstairs dead?" Blanco dropped the chicken leg onto the plate, wiped his mouth and hands, and said, "Thank you, Pierre. Sorry for our loss." He got up and left the room.

"My Nancy? Upstairs? Eric didn't say where they were found. What did he mean by that?" thought Blanco. "My Nancy? She was in bed with Philip. Interesting. Greed, Anger, Maybe Jealousy?" He went back upstairs. Officer Phelps was taking statements. "Hey, Phelps, can you collect the statements from the Staff? Please. I want to look them over. I want to see Pierre's statement also."

"Yes, Sir. I'll get on it right away."

Dr. Rojas arrived, and his team dusted the room and took photos. Blanco went to the photographer Ed Gorski. "Hi Ed, There is a secret passage on the left side of the fireplace. I was in there and found footprints on the dusty floor. Can you get me some photos of those? You know the deal. Be careful; those could be a key to who is behind all this."

"Sure thing. Detective."

Going over to Dr. Rojas, "Hey Doc, What do you think?"

"Have to get them back to the lab to look closer, but it looks pretty much the same to me, Sam. Got any leads?"

"Going in lots of directions. Maybe the footprints in the dust will open something up."

"We have it from here, Sam."

"Good, I'll be downstairs. See you later, Doc."

"Oh, by the way, Sam, the Tweed woman was very intoxicated." Blanco shrugged, "Thanks, Doc."

He retrieved the book from his car and went back to the Study. Placing it on the desk, he sat down. The cover alone was intimidating, sending an eerie chill down his spine. "What secrets are you hiding in here?" he asked. Opening the book, he encountered the first roadblock. It was written in some strange language, filled with unrecognizable symbols and meticulously hand-printed inscriptions. The pages were adorned with graphics depicting creatures and armored men in battle, while others showed hordes of figures with their arms raised, seemingly worshiping a pyramid-shaped structure emitting beams of light in all directions. Some pages even displayed gruesome scenes of torture and the slaughter of naked women. "Could this group have a hand in all of this?" he wondered aloud. He went back downstairs.

Chapter Nine

Mr. Ginsberg was preparing for the reading of the will as he sat on the couch, facing the arched windows overlooking the moonlit gardens. The full moon cast its white glow upon the fountain and statues, creating an eerie ambiance. Suddenly, he was struck on the side of the head, knocking him off the couch and sending his paperwork scattering all around. The scarlet liquid of life flowed onto the floor from his head wound.

Simone and Claude walked together in the hallway, and she nervously spoke up. "Please stay with me tonight." Claude responded reassuringly, "It will be my pleasure, Simone." She began to relax and managed a forced smile. "Come on; I'll take you to your room." Simone implored, "Don't leave me, Claude." He replied firmly, "Not a chance," providing her with comfort and security.

Officer Phelps knocked on the Study door, but Blanco was absent, so he entered the room. As he approached the desk, he noticed the book. "What's this?" he wondered, opening the cover. "Holy Moley! This is creepy stuff." Out of nowhere, he was struck on the side of the head from behind, dropping to his knees. Phelps struggled to get up, reaching for his assailant, only to be bludgeoned again. His lifeless body crumpled to the floor. The attacker then slipped out of the room through the secret passage next to the fireplace, taking the ominous volume and all the collected statements with them.

Lester was in his suite, tending to his bruises and enjoying a soak in the tub. He hadn't heard any commotion in the hallway and was lost in dreams of his impending new life – traveling to beautiful places, getting a fancy car, and a world full of new opportunities. Suddenly, he heard a noise coming from the other room. He shouted, "Who's there? What do you want? Can't I have some privacy?" Receiving no response, he grabbed a towel, exited the tub, and entered the bedroom. To his surprise, no one was there. Shrugging it off, he walked to the corner of the room, pulled the tapestry, and summoned the Chambermaid for dinner as he got dressed.

A few moments later, Carol knocked at the door. Lester opened it, concerned by the look of distress on her face. He asked, "Are you okay? You look like you've been crying. Come in. Can I do anything to help?" Carol replied, "No, Sir." Lester inquired further, "Why are you so sad?" She delivered the heartbreaking news, "Don't you know that they found Philip and Nancy murdered?" Lester was taken aback, "What? When? How?" Carol continued, "The police and coroners are all over the mansion trying to figure it out." Overwhelmed with grief, she began to cry. Lester, out of character, held her in comfort, not knowing how to console her. He suggested, "Come, sit here on the couch. Can I get you some water?" Carol hesitated, then replied, "Sir, I'm supposed to serve you tonight."

"Relax Carol, relax." Lester, still shaken, tried to provide some solace.

Blanco descended the stairs, and the mansion was abuzz with activity. Officer French approached him with a rolled-up canvas. "Hey, Detective, I'm glad you're back. We found this map. It looks complicated, but it's not." He opened the document, revealing a diagram of all the passages leading away from the central hub. Blanco was impressed, "This is great, French. Where did you find it?" French explained, "There was a false bottom in the podium, Sir." Blanco appreciated the discovery, "This is amazing, French.

How many passages have you covered so far?" French replied, "About 28, all leading to different mansions, Sir." Blanco acknowledged his efforts, "This is going to take some time. Good work, French."

"Listen, they found two more bodies upstairs. Keep an eye out for anything suspicious," Blanco instructed. "Yes, Sir," came the swift reply.

In need of a clear mind, Blanco left and headed home to Christina. When he entered, he found her asleep on the couch with the TV still on. Gently touching her shoulder, he called out, "Hey, Sleeping Beauty, your Prince is home." She opened her eyes and, in a groggy voice, greeted him, "Hello, my Prince," before pulling him down onto the floor. There, they made love, their passion evident as they pleasured each other. Christina was always eager to please her man, and Sam couldn't help but express his gratitude. "I must be the luckiest guy in the world to have such a beautiful, loving, devoted wife. I love you, Christina." They lay in each other's arms for a brief moment before retiring to bed.

The following day, Sam rose early and stepped into the shower, positioning himself facing the showerhead with his hands against the wall. As the water cascaded over him, he found solace in its comforting embrace, allowing his thoughts to flow freely. "Pierre is my number one suspect. His comments, the 'My Nancy!' remark. And how did he know the bodies were upstairs? Number two is Eric; he has motive. If the Mansion is sold, he'll be out of a job and a place to live.

Number three, Dominata, a potential exposé of a secret society. And number four, Lester Coonz. He's always been a peculiar one." Lost in contemplation, Sam felt Christina's arms wrap around him, her soapy hands gliding over his body, providing a sensual massage that stirred his desire. He savored her touch, turning to face her. With her wet hair clinging to her exquisite figure, he couldn't help but question reality. "Am I dreaming?" he marveled. In response, she turned and pressed herself against him, initiating a rhythmic dance of love. They continued their intimate connection until the water turned cold. Chuckling in the sexiest way, Christina led him back to the bedroom, where they surrendered to their passion until exhaustion claimed them.

Eric and the staff were busy preparing breakfast. Pierre worked diligently at the stove, while chambermaids set up the dining room. Meanwhile, Joseph conducted room inspections upstairs and notified the guests that breakfast would be served at 9:30. William, responsible for checking the lower levels, made a shocking discovery in the Study. He found Officer Phelps' lifeless body behind the desk and immediately rushed to the kitchen to inform Mr. Klaus.

"Mr. Klaus! Mr. Kraus! There's a dead officer in the Study!" William's voice trembled, and he was visibly shaken. Eric and David quickly followed William to the Study, leaving the chambermaids huddled together in fear. Pierre, on the other hand, continued to cook, seemingly unfazed by the news.

Joseph completed his room inspections and returned to the kitchen. Fran informed him about the situation in the Study. Joseph couldn't hide his concern as he sat down, trying to steady himself. Eric remained composed, while David stood quietly by his side. Eric made the necessary call to the police once again.

"This is Eric Klaus calling once more. We have a deceased police officer in the Study. Please notify Detective Blanco, and I'll inform the officers here."

Blanco reached for the bedside phone and answered, "Blanco." He listened intently to the message and then said with a sense of urgency, "I'm on my way."

"Oh, Sweety," Christina said, her disappointment evident in her soft voice. "Round 3?"

"I have to go," Blanco replied, bending down to kiss her. The phone rang again, and he quickly picked it up, saying, "Blanco."

"Captain Lockhart here, Sam," came the stern voice on the other end of the line. "What's happening at the Van Cleese house? It seems you have a lot of help over there, and now a dead officer?

I need an explanation, Sam. I have residents complaining of privacy invasions. What the hell are you into there?"

"It's been three days of hell, Sir," Blanco explained, frustration in his tone. "I have seven bodies, I know of twenty or more suspects, and a map of almost fifty locations. I'm on my way there now, Sir."

"I'll meet you there, Sam," Captain Lockhart replied firmly.

"Yes, Sir. Thank you," Blanco acknowledged before hanging up the phone.

Once the officers were informed of Phelps's death, a mixture of sadness and anger swept through them. The loss of one of their own fueled their determination to bring whoever was responsible to justice. With a renewed sense of purpose, they continued their search for clues.

Chapter Ten

Lester awoke, finding Carol nestled in his arms. She had spent the entire night sleeping by his side. As she opened her eyes, he greeted her with a smile. "Good morning." Carol blushed and quickly apologized, attempting to get up. Lester reassured her, "Carol, it's okay. Stay here with me." He extended his arms, inviting her closer. Confused yet intrigued, Carol hesitated before slowly returning to his embrace. Their lips met in a tender, passionate kiss as they moved to the couch. Lester had never experienced such warmth from a woman before. Their lovemaking was gentle and sensitive, each kiss deepening their connection.

Carol's attentiveness and thrilling presence delighted Lester in ways he couldn't put into words. As they held each other, the intensity peaked, and they found solace in one another. He kissed her and whispered, "Carol, you are indescribable." She held him tightly, resting her head against his chest.

Simone awoke in her bed and noticed Claude lying on the chaise lounge near the window. Clad in a sheet, she approached him, observing his well-toned physique with admiration. "Hmm," she thought, "you've been keeping that well hidden." As the sunlight streamed in, Claude stirred, and she turned to leave. "Hey there, can I help you?" he called out, his smile evident as he reached up to grab the sheet. Simone hesitated for a moment, then greeted him with a smile. "Good morning."

With a playful gesture, she let go of the sheet, revealing her perfectly sculpted body, radiating like a goddess in the sunlight. Claude sat up on the chaise as she drew closer, lifting her in his arms and carrying her to the bed. They shared passionate kisses, intensifying their connection as he gently laid her down beside him. Breathlessly, he asked, "What brought this on?" She giggled and replied, "It must have been the sunlight." Fuelled by desire, they made love fiercely and impulsively, consumed by each other's presence, until they reached a powerful climax.

"Wow! That was pretty intense," he gasped.

"You haven't seen anything yet," she playfully teased, jumping out of bed and leading him towards the bathroom. "Want to take a shower together?"

Joseph went from room to room, dutifully announcing Breakfast at 9:30. When he reached Lester's suite, he knocked and made the announcement. Carol, who was in the room, froze with worry.

"What do I do?" she asked anxiously. "They must be looking for me."

Lester, sitting up in bed, reassured her, saying, "Calm down, My Love. It will be fine." He looked into her eyes and affectionately called her "My Love."

Surprised, Carol replied, "My Love? I have never met anyone like you, Carol. You are not just a fling. It has meaning to me. I want to be with you."

Feeling uncertain, Carol questioned him, "But you don't know anything about me."

Lester responded sincerely, "So sit with me and tell me everything about you." Carol continued to gaze into his eyes, contemplating his words.

"Why me?" she finally asked, her curiosity evident. "You have everything. Why me?"

Lester paused for a moment, collecting his thoughts. "Because meeting you changed me," he admitted. "I have always been selfish, greedy, and ruthless. But you made me care for the first time in my life."

Realizing the urgency of the situation, Carol hurriedly got dressed, saying, "I have to go. They'll be looking for me."

Lester nodded understandingly and pleaded, "Come back to me later, OK?" Carol shyly nodded in agreement and swiftly left the room.

After Carol's departure, Lester took a shower and made his way down to the dining room, joining the others for breakfast.

After taking an intense shower, Simone and Claude quickly dressed and made their way to the dining room for breakfast. Upon entering, they were greeted by Lester, who wore a big smile on his face.

"Good morning!" Lester exclaimed cheerfully. Confused, Simone and Claude exchanged glances. Simone responded, "Good morning, Lester. You seem unusually happy today, considering everything that has happened here in the past few days. Are you anxious about the will?"

Lester's smile faltered for a moment as he realized he had forgotten about the will. "Oh, yes. The will. I almost forgot. Do you know what time the reading is?" he questioned.

Simone shook her head. "I'm not sure. Where is Mr. Ginsberg?" Claude inquired.

Meanwhile, they were already seated at the table, enjoying their servings of Eggs Benedict accompanied by a variety of fruits and melons. Carol entered the room carrying a tray of coffee. As she poured coffee for the guests, Lester sat up eagerly.

Curious, Claude asked Lester, "What happened to you yesterday, Lester?"

Lester glanced at Carol, who blushed and turned away. "You wouldn't believe me if I told you. I had a little setback, but later it turned into something wonderful," he replied cryptically.

Simone interjected, her tone filled with concern, "How can anything be wonderful when two people were found dead down the hall from you? And two more the day before, not to mention poor Ms. Tweed and the police officer?"

Lester sighed, expressing his remorse. "I feel terrible about everything that has happened. But sometimes sorrow brings people closer together," he stated.

As they continued their meal, Claude announced his intention to find out the time of the will reading. Turning to Simone, he asked, "Where should I meet you?"

Simone contemplated for a moment before responding, "I think I want to take a walk in the gardens. I have so many mixed emotions right now."

Lester chimed in, offering, "I'll join you to go see Mr. Ginsberg."

Leaving the room together, Lester glanced at Carol and whispered, "Come to my room when you can get away." She responded with a smile.

Captain Lockhart and Blanco met outside by the front fountain.

"Good morning, sir," Blanco greeted.

"Morning, Blanco. So, what kind of craziness is happening here?" Captain Lockhart inquired.

As they entered the vestibule, Claude suddenly shouted, "Mr. Ginsberg is dead! Get the police! Ginsberg is dead!"

Alarmed, Captain Lockhart and Blanco rushed up the stairs, followed by two officers, Troy Lake and Steve Wilson, as well as other staff members who had heard the commotion.

Blanco asked Claude, "What happened here?"

"We went to see Ginsberg about the time of the reading and found him on the floor," Claude explained.

"Wait out there," Blanco instructed the officers and staff members who had gathered. He and Captain Lockhart proceeded into the room to find Ginsberg lying face down, with blood-soaked pages scattered around him. Their gaze fell upon the fire poker lying on the floor near the fireplace.

"This one is different, sir. There was nothing left behind in the other cases," Blanco remarked.

Captain Lockhart pondered the situation. "So, who would want this man dead, Sam?"

"Whoever would benefit the most from the delay in the will reading. Eric Klaus, Pierre LaMonte, and the staff," Sam replied.

Soon, Dr. Rojas and his team arrived to examine Officer Phelps, who had been injured earlier, and now to observe Mr. Ginsberg's body.

"Detective, we have two very different wounds here. I will further examine them in the lab, but from my initial assessment, it appears there was more than one assailant," Dr. Rojas informed.

Confused, Captain Lockhart asked, "What do you mean, Doc?"

"Mr. Ginsberg was struck with the poker, and I hope the team recovers some fingerprints. Officer Phelps was struck by a blunt object, possibly a bat or club, similar to Thomas the Butler's injuries. The interesting thing is that they were both hit from the right side. All our previous victims were struck from the left," Dr. Rojas explained.

Realization dawned on Captain Lockhart. "So, you're saying we might have two, maybe three killers?"

"In all my years, I have never seen anything like this," Captain Lockhart exclaimed. "We need to talk to the most suspicious person first. Come on, Blanco. Let's go see this Pierre guy."

Pierre stood in the kitchen, slicing a ham, as the men entered.

"Detective, it seems like you have your hands full. And you, sir, are?" Pierre inquired.

"I'm Captain Lockhart, and you must be Chef Pierre," Captain Lockhart introduced himself.

"That I am," Pierre confirmed.

"Do you mind if I ask you some questions?" Captain Lockhart requested.

"Certainly not," Pierre agreed.

"How well did you know Nancy Gains, Mr. LaMonte?" Captain Lockhart inquired.

Pierre looked at him curiously. "I knew her as well as any of the others."

"What about Linda Stokes?" Captain Lockhart continued probing.

"About the same," Pierre replied.

Captain Lockhart proceeded to question Pierre further. "Have you ever had or are you currently having any relations with any female staff?"

Pierre appeared uncomfortable. "What are you saying, Captain?"

"Are you involved with any of the female staff here?" Captain Lockhart clarified.

Pierre's discomfort grew. "I don't know what you mean. They are all special to me. We work closely every day."

"Some closer than others, Mr. LaMonte?" Captain Lockhart pressed.

• • •

Pierre's surprise at Nancy's death caught Captain Lockhart's attention. "You said, 'My Nancy!' What did you mean by that?"

"They are all my girls. I love them all," Pierre explained.

Captain Lockhart continued his line of questioning. "What about Linda Stokes? Did you love her too?"

Pierre hesitated before responding, "Ah, Linda? She was special."

"Really? How special, Mr. LaMonte?" Captain Lockhart probed further.

Pierre admitted, "She was the most beautiful."

Meanwhile, Blanco walked over to the prep area, observing his surroundings. As Pierre grew more agitated, Blanco noticed something. "Southpaw?"

Confused, Pierre asked, "What is that, sir?"

"You're left-handed," Blanco pointed out.

Pierre confirmed, "Why yes, sir."

As Blanco moved around, he noticed a wooden mallet with a flat side and little pyramid shapes on the other face. "What is this, Mr. LaMonte?"

Pierre nervously explained, "That is a meat tenderizing tool."

Blanco made a decision. "I have to take this in for testing," he stated, wrapping the tool in a towel.

"Oh, by the way, Mr. LaMonte, how did you know that Philip and Nancy were upstairs?" Blanco questioned.

Pierre remained silent. The men left the room, instructing Pierre, "Don't go far, Mr. LaMonte."

In the vestibule, Captain Lockhart addressed Sam. "I think we have something here, Sam."

• • •

"Let me take you down into the tunnel area, sir," Blanco offered.

Upon their arrival, Captain Lockhart and Blanco were greeted by Officer French.

"Good to see you, Captain," Officer French greeted.

"How are you, French? What's going on here?" Captain Lockhart inquired.

"We've been searching the tunnels, sir. We have a map, and many of them connect with mansions in the area. We also found this," Officer French explained. He walked over to an evidence table and presented a book containing names of cult practitioners. "Look at this, sir."

He handed the registry to Captain Lockhart and Blanco. The book contained hundreds of names.

"Where did you find this, French?" Blanco asked.

"On the back wall of the altar, behind the podium, sir. There is a golden door with a safe," Officer French revealed.

Blanco quickly skimmed over the names: Lynquest, Pinkerton, Maryweather, Frost, Bradhurst, Wellington. Many of the wealthiest families in Newport.

"This is a major find, sir. Could this have any bearing on the murders?" Blanco pondered.

"I don't know, Sam, but we must handle this very delicately," Captain Lockhart responded.

In another scene, Pierre was in his room when he heard a knock at the door. He opened it to find Audrey and Carmen standing there, smiling. He graciously stepped aside and bowed, inviting them inside.

"Good afternoon, my sweets," Pierre greeted as he closed the door. The three of them came together in a passionate embrace, kissing and exploring each other's bodies. Pierre's skill in carnal pleasure was evident as he attended to both women with equal care and attention.

"May I offer you some wine?" Pierre offered as he moved towards the wine rack, uncorking a bottle of Rosé and pouring three glasses. The women sat on a long couch, eagerly awaiting their libations.

Sitting between them, they raised their glasses in a toast, commemorating their secret rendezvous of forbidden love. Audrey, with her long, wavy red hair, had bright blue eyes and fair, milky-white skin. She possessed ample curves, her breasts full and voluptuous. In contrast, Carmen had dark skin, captivating black eyes, and silky, flowing black hair. She exuded strength, with a toned physique and smaller breasts. They were almost complete opposites, drawn together by desire.

Pierre, with a satisfied smile, set his wine glass down and reclined on the couch. As if following a script, the ladies began undressing him, their hands lightly caressing his body, their eyes locked onto his. Excitement surged through him. Rising to their feet, they kissed and sensually explored each other as they shed their garments. Pierre watched with mounting anticipation.

Now naked, they returned to him, one on each side. Their lips met his, their hands roaming freely over his body. They kissed each other passionately, their hands tenderly cupping their breasts. Moving down, they lavished him with attention, sharing in his arousal. Wine cascaded over him as they licked and pleasured him from every angle, creating an oral symphony of ecstasy.

Pierre stood before them, captivated by their enchantment. Taking their hands, he led them to his bed. There, they engaged in a mesmerizing three-way dance of unrestrained passion, each experiencing the ultimate pleasures the others had to offer. At no moment was one left untouched by the delightful bliss bestowed upon them. The intimacy continued unabated, a never-ending journey of insatiable desire. Pierre's hunger knew no bounds, and the ladies matched his voracity for promiscuity.

⁂

The culmination arrived in a crescendo of convulsive ecstasy as they climaxed together, their bodies intertwined in the throes of intense release. They held each other tightly, trembling in the aftermath of their shared ecstasy.

* * *

Chapter Eleven

Blanco and Captain Lockhart entered the vestibule, ready to leave, when Joseph the Butler informed them that Dr. Rojas was on the phone.

"Excuse me, Captain," Blanco went to take the call. "Dr. Rojas, how can I help you?"

"Hi Sam, I did tests on the tenderizing tool and found traces of human blood; also, the pyramid pattern on the face matches the wounds on Philip Jenkins, Nancy Gains, Linda Stokes, and Trey Wilson. It looks like you have one real suspect. Still working on the other things. Ed Gorski has some photos of the footprints for you."

"That's great, Doc. Thank you."

Blanco returned to the vestibule, "Captain, we have a match on the mallet. We have to arrest Pierre LaMonte in connection with the four murders. The wounds match with human blood traces."

"Well, let's go get him, Detective."

They proceeded through the kitchen to the servant quarters and asked Fran, the handmaiden, for Pierre's room location. "It's just around the corner, Sir. Number 11."

Blanco knocked on the door, but there was no answer again, and Pierre opened it, standing there in a towel. His hair was disheveled, and he reeked of the smell of sex.

"Detective? What are you doing here?"

"May we come in, Mr. LaMonte?"

"Why? No! You may not..."

By that time, Audrey and Carmen were up and getting dressed.

"Mr. LaMonte, you are under arrest for the murders of Linda Stokes, Trey Wilson, Philip Jenkins, and Nancy Gains. Anything you say can and will be used against you in court. If you do not have an attorney, one can be appointed for you."

"What are you saying?"

They entered the room, turned him around, and placed handcuffs on him. Audrey and Carmen stood in disbelief as Pierre was escorted through the house to Blanco's big black Mercury. The towel fell to the ground, and Captain Lockhart picked it up and placed it on Pierre's lap.

"Good work, Detective."

"That's one, Captain, maybe two or more to go."

Eric rushed in through the front door, his voice filled with concern. "What is the meaning of this? What is happening here? You can't just arrest my Chef!"

Blanco remained firm, his tone unwavering. "Mr. Klaus, you once mentioned that you were the Housekeeping Manager. Well, now, sir, it's time for you to manage."

Confused, Eric responded, "Excuse me, Detective."

Blanco pressed on, undeterred. "Your shoes, Mr. Klaus. What size are they?"

Eric paused, taken aback by the unexpected question. "Eight and a half, sir."

Without another word, Eric turned and retreated into the house. Blanco acknowledged the successful outcome. "Good work, Sam."

"Thanks, Captain," Sam replied gratefully. He proceeded to escort Pierre to the police station, where he went through the necessary procedures: checking him in, providing him with an orange jumpsuit, and placing him in a holding cell. Throughout the entire process, Pierre remained silent, keeping his head down. Blanco concluded his duties for the day and headed home.

Meanwhile, in the kitchen, Eric called William to relay an important message. "Please inform the remaining guests that lunch will be served at 2." As he worked, Eric prepared ham finger sandwiches and cut fruit. The staff couldn't help but discuss the recent arrest and everything that had unfolded. The tension in the air was palpable. "This is awful. I'm scared wherever I go," one staff member expressed. Another chimed in, "We all are. We need to stick together."

Simone and Claude took a leisurely stroll across the estate, always within sight of a watchful officer. Their relationship was growing stronger by the day. At the same time, Lester and Carol's connection was heating up as well. Carol visited Lester's suite to inform him about lunch at 2, but their interaction quickly turned into an intense, spontaneous moment of passion. They became consumed by a lustful frenzy. Lester showered Carol with kisses, pulling her towards his bed as she fumbled to undo his trousers. With passion and urgency, she straddled him, their bodies moving in sync. Lester experienced a level of pleasure he had never known before. Their climax was explosive, and they lay together, gazing up at the canopy above them.

"I love you, Lester," Carol whispered, her voice filled with adoration.

Lester, breathless and overwhelmed, replied, "You are incredible, my love."

⁕ ⁕ ⁕

"You bring out the best in me, Lester," Carol confided, basking in the afterglow of their intimate encounter.

Chapter Twelve

Blanco concluded his duties for the day and headed home. In the yard, Christina relaxed on a lounge chair, wearing a bathing suit top and shorts. As she soaked up the sun, Blanco stood before her, blocking her sunlight. Christina opened her eyes and playfully remarked, "Hey, handsome, you're in my light."

Blanco challenged her, "What are you going to do about it, lady?"

In response, Christina raised her leg and placed her foot on his chest. Blanco gently held her foot as if cradling a baby chick, kissing each toe lovingly while caressing her calf. He suggested, "What do you say we continue this inside, ma'am?" Christina giggled in delight.

Meanwhile, Carol announced her departure, saying, "I have to go for now. I'll be back tonight, okay?"

"Until later, my love," Lester replied. Carol left the room to attend to her daily duties, proceeding downstairs to dust and freshen up the lower-level rooms.

Approaching 2 p.m., Simone and Claude made their way to the dining room, while Lester tidied up before joining them. A limousine arrived, carrying Hiram Shwartzcoff from the law office.

Eric greeted him at the door, extending a warm welcome and hoping for an end to the ongoing chaos. "Mr. Shwartzcoff, lunch is served at two if you would like to dine."

"I want to speak with the remaining heirs; thank you," Hiram replied.

The staff members were on edge, expressing their frustrations. "Not knowing what's happening is driving me crazy," one of them voiced. David paced anxiously in the kitchen. "Arresting Pierre for the murders? Eight people dead in just a few days! It's insanity. I'm frightened."

Acknowledging the fear that gripped them all, another staff member replied, "You're right, David. We're all scared. But what can we do?"

Joseph chimed in, "We are all forced to stay here, and it's not safe, even with all the police presence."

Alice added, "We just have to watch out for one another, as best we can."

William concluded, "Indeed, we must look out for one another during these uncertain times."

The phone rang, piercing the tranquility of the Blanco residence. Sam and Christina, lying in bed after a passionate afternoon, shifted their attention to the call. Sam picked up the phone, while Christina got up to prepare some food. "Blanco, can I help you?" Sam inquired.

"Hi, Detective, Sergeant Syms here. Ed Gorski said he could drop off the photos at the Mansion later today," Syms informed.

"That's great, Syms. I'll be there after four," Sam replied. He then moved into the kitchen, admiring Christina's beauty as she made a salad. Overwhelmed by love, he approached her from behind and wrapped his arms around her, gently cupping her breasts. "I just want to tell you how much you mean to me. I love you, Christina," he expressed.

Christina leaned into him with affection. "I love you, Sam," she reciprocated.

In the dining room, Hiram Shwartzcoff entered, where the three remaining heirs were already seated at the expansive table. "Good afternoon. My name is Hiram Shwartzcoff. I am representing the Estate of Sir Andrew Van Cleese following the untimely passing of Mr. Ginsberg," he introduced himself. "Due to these unusual circumstances, there will be a delayed reading of the will. I cannot predict a time frame as there have been many revisions. Your patience is appreciated." With that, he settled at the far end of the table, away from the trio.

"Great!" Lester exclaimed. "What do we do now?"

"You heard Blanco. We can't leave yet," Claude added.

Simone chimed in, "We wait it out. We are all in danger, but if we stay close, we might be okay. Blanco and the police have made progress with the arrest."

"Let's eat!" Claude suggested, grabbing a few sandwiches.

Elsewhere, Officer French organized a list of names from the registry. He intended to discuss with Blanco the possibility of conducting door-to-door interviews to gather information about Dominata.

Chapter Thirteen

Blanco made a stop at the Station House before returning to the Mansion. He wanted to apply pressure on Pierre, perhaps even elicit a confession. Officer Gonzales escorted Pierre into the interrogation room, securing his cuffed hands to the table. Blanco entered, carrying a large file which he promptly dropped on the table, employing a tactic to intimidate Pierre. "So, where are we going with this, Mr. Lamonte?" he inquired.

"I did not do these things, Detective," Pierre pleaded, his hands open in a desperate gesture.

Blanco leaned in, maintaining his stern demeanor. "We have evidence of human blood on the murder weapon—your meat tenderizer, Mr. LaMonte."

Glancing down at Pierre's open palms, Blanco noticed a sizable bandage on his right hand. "What happened to your hand, Mr. LaMonte?"

"I cut it. I'm a chef, Detective. We sometimes get cut," Pierre explained.

Blanco inspected the bandage closely. "That looks pretty bad."

"Yes, it was deep, with blood everywhere in my station," Pierre confirmed.

"Mr. LaMonte, how many meat tenderizers do you have in the kitchen?" Blanco inquired.

"Three, maybe four. When I started working for Sir Andrew as the head chef, I had sous chefs who assisted me. We used to have big parties, and the kitchen was always bustling. But now, it's just me," Pierre revealed.

"That's all for now, Mr. LaMonte," Blanco concluded, rising from his seat and exiting the room.

"I need to find those mallets," Blanco thought to himself as he returned to the Mansion. He headed to the phone and dialed Captain Lockhart's number. "Good evening, sir. I need search warrants to go through all the servants' quarters. I have reason to believe that Pierre may not be our man," Blanco requested.

"I'll get you what you need, Sam," Captain Lockhart assured him.

Meanwhile, Carol entered the music room, humming to herself as she dusted the furniture. Lost in her thoughts about Lester, she walked past a large window. Suddenly, Fran emerged from behind the draperies, startling Carol. "What are you doing in here?" Carol asked, taken aback.

Fran's eyes had a glazed look, and her face contorted into an evil snarl. "You betrayed him! You whore! You belonged to him. We all belong to him! We love him. He loves us and cares for us. How could you do that to him? To us?" Fran ranted, her emotions spiraling out of control. Without warning, she lunged at Carol, swinging the mallet gripped in her left hand, grazing Carol's forehead. As Carol tried to duck and escape, she was struck again, this time on her shoulder. Crying out for help, she was met with a final fatal blow to the top of her head.

Fran's body surged with adrenaline as she dragged Carol's lifeless form toward the window, concealing her behind the draperies. Adjusting her own appearance, Fran carefully tucked the mallet under her apron and stealthily left the room. Once in her own quarters, she swiftly undressed and stepped into the shower, meticulously washing away any traces of blood from the mallet. "I punished her, Pierre. She was a slut, just like the others. You are the love of our lives. I can't allow them to betray our love, and I will NOT!" she declared fervently. Adorning the walls surrounding her dressing mirror were photographs, news clippings, and magazine articles showcasing Pierre's remarkable culinary achievements and numerous accolades from around the world. Fran took the mallet, wrapped it in a hand towel, and discreetly placed it in the bottom drawer.

Meanwhile, Blanco was en route to the tunnels when Eric intercepted him, holding out an envelope. "Mr. Gorski left this for you, Detective," Eric informed him.

"Thank you, Mr. Klaus. By the way, what kind of shoes do you wear?" Blanco inquired.

"Why, they're Klogs, sir. We all wear them," Eric replied with a smile.

Blanco proceeded to the library and carefully opened the envelope. Inside, he discovered a series of photographs and a detailed description. The words were prominently displayed in large letters: "Chuck Taylor Converse - classic sole pattern, ¾-inch perforated diagonal diamond squares with perforated centers."

Chapter Fourteen

Back in the tunnels, Blanco engaged in conversation with Officer French. "You've been working really hard down here, French. I think it's time we start reaching out to the families associated with these tunnels," Blanco suggested.

"I was thinking the same thing, Detective. I've compiled a preliminary list of names from the registry," French replied.

"Let's wrap things up down here tonight and begin our door-to-door inquiries tomorrow. Thank you, French," Blanco acknowledged gratefully.

Ascending the stairs, Blanco entered the kitchen where William and David were engaged in conversation. "Gentlemen, may I have a look around?" Blanco requested.

"Of course, Detective," William and David responded in unison.

"Where is Eric?" Blanco inquired.

"He may be in his chambers, sir," David informed him.

Discreetly observing their footwear, Blanco noted, "Klogs," he thought to himself. "May I ask, does the staff generally wear the same uniforms? The butlers in tuxedos, the handmaids in matching dresses and aprons? And what about shoes? What kind of shoes do you all wear?" Blanco questioned.

"Well, sir, the most comfortable option is Klogs. We're on our feet all day and night, and they provide the best quality. Everyone wears them, even the ladies," David explained.

Blanco thoroughly inspected the kitchen, examining various equipment and utensils. He picked up knives, strainers, and whisks. Turning his attention back to the conversation, he asked, "Were you present when Mr. LaMonte cut himself?"

"Oh yes, sir. I was here," David confirmed. "It was quite a gusher—blood everywhere, all over the workspace. Eventually, he tightly wrapped the wound and went to the hospital for stitches. It took Fran and Alice quite some time to clean up. You have to hand it to him, though. He came back and cooked dinner for all of us."

"Thank you, gentlemen," Blanco expressed his gratitude before exiting the kitchen.

Blanco approached Eric's door and knocked. "Who is it?" came the voice from inside. "It's Detective Blanco, Mr. Klaus. May I have a few words with you?" The door opened, revealing a nervous Eric. "What can I help you with, Detective?" he asked.

"We found a very old book, Mr. Klaus. Now, you've worked here for many years, correct?" Blanco inquired.

"Yes, Detective, 50 years," Eric confirmed.

"Tell me, Mr. Klaus, what do you know about Dominata?" Blanco questioned.

"Dominata? Sir, 1 know nothing of Dominata," Eric responded.

"Sir Andrew was a very wealthy and powerful man. Beneath this mansion, there are a number of tunnels extending from a central room directly underneath us. And you're telling me that after 50 years, you know nothing of Dominata? What are you hiding, Mr. Klaus?" Blanco pressed, noticing Eric's nervous pacing.

"We've had many events here over the years—grand parties, dinners. People from all over the world would attend. I've never been down under this house. I didn't want to go. I didn't want to know. There is access from some of the rooms on the main floor. The passages in all the upper suites connect and descend. After the gatherings, when the guests would retire for the evening, I don't know what went on," Eric divulged.

"Where will you go from here, Mr. Klaus?" Blanco asked, his voice softening.

"I don't know, Detective. I don't know," Eric replied, lowering his head.

"Thank you, Mr. Klaus," Blanco acknowledged before leaving. He made a stop in the kitchen, where Grace, Fran, and Audrey were gathered, busy cutting potatoes, greens, and prepping chickens for dinner service. "Good afternoon, ladies. May I ask you some questions?" Blanco greeted them.

"What can we help you with, Detective?" Grace responded.

"We've already spoken to your officers. You arrested Pierre for murders we know he didn't commit. He is a gentle man, sweet, kind, loving. He would never harm any of us," Fran defended.

Blanco was taken aback by their support. "So if not Mr. LaMonte, then who?" he inquired. Before he could receive an answer, Fran blurted out, "David." The other two women were shocked and tried to silence her. "Yes, David, Detective. He is always lusting after us, peering at us, accidentally touching us inappropriately, and making us feel uncomfortable in his presence. He's jealous of Pierre because we love him."

"Thank you, ladies," Blanco acknowledged, and he headed home, knowing that tomorrow would bring new challenges.

Eric entered the kitchen and announced, "Well, I guess I'm cooking again tonight. Thank you, ladies, for prepping. Dinner is at 7:30. If you could advise our guests."

Simone and Claude returned to her suite after their stroll, while Lester went searching for Carol. Claude went out onto the balcony, gazing at the ocean, as Simone approached him from behind, standing in the doorway. "Claude," she said in a sultry voice, "can you help me with this?" He turned around, captivated by her presence. She stood before him in her bra and panties, her arms behind her back. "I can't seem to unhook this," she teased. Claude's eyes were fixated on her beauty, from head to toe, glistening in the sunlight. He approached her delicately, touching her shoulders as he kissed the back of her neck. She turned around, wrapping her arms around him, and they kissed passionately. Undoing her bra, she stepped back, revealing the flawlessness of her body—silky skin, invitingly round and exquisite breasts. Claude swept her up into his arms, carrying her to the bed, where he kissed her gently and ran his hands lightly over her body. As he barely made contact with her nipples, they hardened in anticipation. He tantalized her with his lips and tongue, exploring the most sensitive areas, while she writhed in delight. Using his fingertips, he rubbed and penetrated her, bringing her to peak after peak of pleasure. She reached for him, whispering, "I want you, Claude." Removing his shorts, she delicately massaged his manhood with her lips and tongue. Together, they exchanged erotic felicities, indulging in a dance of lust and sensual gratification, culminating in a jubilant release as they kissed.

Meanwhile, Lester searched from room to room in his quest to find Carol. Passing Fran in the upstairs hallway, he asked if she had seen Carol. "I need my room tidied up. Have you seen her?" Surprised by the question, Fran replied, "I haven't seen her this afternoon, sir, but if I do, I'll convey your request." "Thank you, Miss," Lester acknowledged before continuing his search.

Mr. Shwartzcoff was busy with paperwork when there was a knock on the door. "Dinner at 7:30, sir," a staff member informed him. He went to the door and requested, "May I take my dinner in my room, please?" William quickly responded, "Yes, sir. I will see to it myself."

By 7:30, Lester still hadn't found Carol and began to grow concerned. Simone and Claude descended the staircase as he approached them. "Hey, guys! Are you going to dinner?" Lester asked. "Hello, Lester. Yes, we're on our way now," Simone replied. "Have you seen Carol on your way?" Lester inquired. "Sorry, we have not. Are you looking for her?" Claude asked. Lester hesitated as Simone and Claude exchanged looks. "You're not looking for room attention at all, are you, Lester?" they chuckled, teasing him. They entered the dining room together.

Blanco, trying to relax while building a suspect list, realized he couldn't hold LaMonte much longer. "The house-to-house starts tomorrow, and they all wear Klogs," he thought to himself. "I have to do a room-by-room search in the morning," Christina suggested. "Dinner, honey." She had prepared a nice tomato sauce with meatballs and sausage. They sat at the table in the dining room, and Blanco expressed, "This here tonight, you and I, together, is why I wanted to retire here." They spent a quiet evening at home, enjoying each other's company.

Chapter Fifteen

French and his officers started their day early, arriving at the Estate of the Bradhurst Family. French drove through one of the tunnels that led directly under the Mansion and knocked on the huge mahogany doors. A butler answered and squinted at French's name tag.

"May I help you, Officer French?" the butler inquired.

French replied, "I'm here on official Police business. I must speak to someone from the Bradhurst family."

The butler informed him, "I'm sorry, Officer, but without an appointment, there is no one you can see."

French insisted, "Just a moment. I'm here on official police business." The butler closed the door momentarily.

As French waited, he marveled at the entrance's splendor and magnificence. It felt like a different world. The door reopened, and the butler announced, "Lady Penelope Bradhurst, Officer French."

Lady Penelope Bradhurst, an elegant woman in her thirties with blonde hair in a bun and blue-grey eyes, stood before him. She was dressed in riding attire, exuding grace and sophistication. French greeted her, "Good morning, Ms. Bradhurst. I am Officer French, and I'm looking into a series of events in a Mansion nearby. May I ask you some questions?"

Lady Penelope, in a rush, replied, "I don't have much time, Officer. As you can see, I'm going out."

French assured her, "I won't keep you too long, Ms. Bradhurst. May I come inside?" The butler intervened, saying, "This way, sir," and led them into a sitting room adjacent to the grand entry hall. The room had a high ceiling, red silk wallpaper with embroidered gold designs, and Provincial-style furniture that lacked comfort. They took a seat across a marble-topped coffee table.

French began his inquiry, "Ms. Bradhurst, have you ever heard of Dominata?"

Lady Penelope paused and asked, "Why are you asking me about Dominata?"

French continued, "Are you aware of a tunnel that begins under this Mansion and connects to a central hub, along with other tunnels?"

Confused, Lady Penelope responded, "Tunnel? What are you talking about? I know nothing of any tunnels, Officer French. What is this about?"

French clarified, "I'm investigating a series of murders that may be connected with the tunnels and Dominata. Anything you can tell me would be of value."

Lady Penelope expressed shock, exclaiming, "Murders? Oh my Lord! I know nothing of this Dominata. I've never had reason to go down to the basement and have never seen anything referring to this Dominata."

French handed her his card and said, "If you think of anything, Ms. Bradhurst, please contact me."

Concerned, Lady Penelope asked, "Should we be concerned about danger from these tunnels?"

French replied honestly, "I can't answer that, ma'am. You are aware of them now."

Back at the Van Cleese Mansion, William was conducting his rounds on the main floor when he entered the music room. The noxious scent of death overwhelmed him as he opened the door. He quickly covered his nose and mouth with a handkerchief and rushed to open the windows. Behind the curtains, he discovered Carol's lifeless body. Overwhelmed by the sight, William stumbled backward, knocking over a coffee table and a vase filled with flowers. As the shock took hold, he vomited while trying to leave the room, accidentally knocking things over in his path. He cried out, "Help! Help! It's Carol! Oh my God! It's Carol!"

The officers and staff quickly responded. Officer Dough Lewis took charge as the repulsive odor permeated into the vestibule. He instructed, "Everyone, please remain calm. We will handle this from here. Troy, can you get Detective Blanco?" Troy acknowledged, "Sure thing, Dough."

Just then, Detective Blanco entered the scene, questioning, "What's happening here?" Officer Lewis informed him, "We have another body, sir."

Blanco reacted with surprise, asking, "What? Where?" Officer Lewis replied, "In the music room, sir." Blanco instructed, "Call Dr. Rojas, gather statements, any witnesses. I want to know where everyone was for the past three days, what they did, and who they were with."

The butler, William, was the one who found Carol's body, prompting Blanco to enter the room, covering his mouth and nose. He approached the body and noticed two blows to the head. Surveying the room, he observed signs of a struggle and traces of William's exit. The staff was in a state of panic, with Marie crying uncontrollably and stating, "None of us are safe here." Fran, sarcastically looking at Blanco, added, "I guess Pierre is innocent." Blanco scowled at her in response.

Dr. Rojas arrived with his team, and Blanco greeted him, saying, "Hey, Sam. What do we have this time?" Sam replied, "She's in the music room, Doc." Dr. Rojas inquired, "Any leads yet?" Blanco shared his suspicions, saying, "I have some suspicions, Doc." Dr.

Rojas expressed hope, "Hope that you can wrap this up soon." Blanco reassured him, "Working on it, Doc."

Lester came running down the stairs. "What's happened? What's going on? Was there another killing?" Eric stopped him, saying, "It's Carol, Sir." Lester cried out, "No! No! Not Carol!" Eric tried to console him as his hysteria erupted. "Who could do such things?" He ranted, "And You!" as he pointed at Blanco. "What are you doing here? It's been a week! Body after body! What are you doing about it? My Carol! Why! Why!"

Blanco approached him. "Mr. Coonz, I'm sorry for this. Did you have some relationship with the deceased?" Lester looked up at him. "We were lovers. I loved her, and she loved me. Why did this happen, Detective? Why?" his voice shrank to a whisper as he covered his face with his hands.

Blanco thought, "What is the common thread connecting these killings? Five staff, three guests, and a police officer. I have to figure this out." As he headed to the study.

Officer French drove up to the Lynquist Estate. It was smaller than many but far more elegant, with an enormous fountain with bronze statues of horses on their hind legs. He knocked at the doors. Moments later, a butler answered. "May I help you, Officer French?"

"May I speak to the Master of the house?"

"That would be Sir Martin. Sir. He is unable to speak to you, Sir. Sadly, Sir Martin is bedridden."

"Can I go up and see him? I'm investigating a group called Dominata. Do you know of such a group?"

"Why yes, I do, Officer."

French reached into his rear pocket for his notepad. "What is your name? Sir."

"I'm Greyson Tibbs, Sir. With two B's."

"Tell me what you know. Mr. Tibbs."

"Years ago, Sir Martin and several other nearby residents would meet regularly at the Van Cleese chateau. Wealthy people from all over the world would visit. It is said that tunnels connect a series of mansions to a chamber where they would collaborate on ventures."

"What kind of ventures? Mr. Tibbs."

"I wouldn't know that, Sir. They were secret meetings."

"How long ago were these meetings, Mr. Tibbs."

"Oh, Sir Martin is in his nineties, Officer. It had to be at least 10 or 15 years ago."

"So you are saying?"

"I don't think Dominata exists anymore. I know Sir Martin certainly doesn't attend."

"Thank you, Mr. Tibbs."

Blanco began his room-by-room search, starting with David's rooms. He remembered what Fran had said and was extra cautious as David stood by during the investigation. Blanco went through the drawers, under the mattress, in closets, and in the bathroom. He found nothing but some adult magazines.

Next was Joseph, a taciturn man. His room was spotless; everything was in order. His clothes were neatly folded, and his shoes (Klogs) were placed in a row, almost like a military inspection. Blanco found nothing suspicious.

William's room was also neat, with nothing out of the ordinary to be seen.

Eric Klaus followed, and Blanco took his time, sensing that something might turn up. Eric stood nervously by as Blanco searched. Blanco was slowly going through the drawers, finding Eric to be very organized. His room was more extensive than the others, with large windows providing ample light. When Blanco reached the closet, he found suits and shirts neatly hung. Eric became more agitated as Blanco examined his belongings, especially when he looked at the shoes. There were four pairs: three pairs of Klogs and one pair of Chuck Taylor Converse.

Blanco picked up the sneakers, and Eric broke down. "I did it! I killed them! I'm the one. I couldn't bear to see the Mansion sold! It's my home. Where would I go?" Blanco said, "Looks like size 8 ½. Are you making a confession, Mr. Klaus?"

Eric was crying. "I killed Mr. Ginsberg in an attempt to delay the will. Then the other murders occurred. I thought they would cover my actions. Thomas was about to find the passages, and I had to stop him. With all the activity in the basement and you having the book, I wanted to protect Sir Andrew's good name. So I tried to take it when Officer Phelps came into the room, almost catching me."

His hands were shaking as he whimpered. "Mr. Klaus, you are under arrest for the murders of Franklin Ginsberg, Thomas Landin, and Officer Darrel Phelps." Blanco turned him around and cuffed him. "You have a right to remain silent; anything you say can and will be used against you in a court of law. You have a right to an attorney, and if you cannot afford one, one will be appointed to you."

He led him through the kitchen and vestibule, to the shock and surprise of all. Blanco called Officer Lewis over. "I want you to take Mr. Klaus here down to the station and book him for three murders: Mr. Ginsberg, Thomas Landin, and Officer Darrel Phelps. I have some more work here. I'll be down at the station later."

"Yes, Sir, Detective. Come along, Mr. Klaus."

Everyone was emotionally upset and confused. Simone and Claude were doing their best to comfort Lester. Dr. Rojas and his team were meticulously searching for clues in the music room, and Mr. Shwartzcoff remained in his suite.

❀ ❀ ❀

Blanco addressed the room, saying, "May I have your attention, please? We have a lot going on here, and I would like all of you to return to your rooms while we sort this out. Mr. Klaus is being held for further questioning. Thank you."

Chapter Sixteen

B lanco began his search with the Handmaidens' rooms. He knocked on Audrey Lange's door. She answered with a smile, her hair down, wearing a long flowered house dress, and her feet bare.

"Come in, Detective. Can I get you some water?" she offered.

"No, thank you, Ms. Lange. I realize this is an uncomfortable time, so I will be as brief as possible," Blanco replied.

"I have nothing to hide, Detective," Audrey assured him.

Blanco meticulously checked closets, and drawers, and then noticed a photo of her and Pierre on top of her dresser.

"Interesting photo, Ms. Lange. Are you close with Mr. LaMonte?" Blanco inquired.

"Well, you may look at it that way. He is very dear to me," she replied.

"Tell me, Ms. Lange, who would have a reason to harm any of the Handmaidens?" Blanco asked.

"I don't know, Detective. I just know it is not Pierre," Audrey responded.

Not finding anything suspicious, Blanco moved on to Carmen Baccia's room and knocked. When she opened the door, her dark eyes were piercing.

"Please don't make a mess, Detective," Carmen cautioned.

"I'll be as quick as I can, Ms. Baccia," Blanco assured her.

Blanco went through Carmen's room in a few minutes but noticed that, like Audrey, she had a photo of herself with Pierre.

"Tell me, Ms. Baccia, what was your relationship with Mr. LaMonte?" Blanco inquired.

"He is wonderful, Detective. We are close," Carmen replied.

Making mental notes and finding nothing questionable, Blanco moved on to Anna Watz, a petite young woman. She was still in her uniform when she opened the door.

"Come in, Detective. Do you think that searching our rooms will turn up the killer? Really?" Anna asked.

"It's standard police protocol, Ms. Watz. I won't be long," Blanco replied.

He walked around Anna's room and found nothing out of order except a photo of her and Pierre. Blanco picked it up.

"Tell me, Ms. Watz, I've seen similar photos in other rooms. Do all the ladies have photos like this with Mr. LaMonte?" he inquired.

Blushing, Anna said, "Pierre is close to all of us. He is an amazing man."

"I see," Blanco acknowledged.

Finding nothing, he moved on to Fran Geller's room. He knocked, but there was no answer. He knocked again, and this time, the door flew open with Fran saying, "I hope you have a warrant to do this."

"I do, Ms. Geller," Blanco replied. She was wearing sweats and slippers. Blanco walked in and instantly noticed her extensive tribute to Pierre – photos, news clips, magazine covers, photos of award ceremonies, and a picture of her with Pierre.

"Looks like you are quite fond of Mr. LaMonte, Ms. Geller," Blanco remarked.

"We have a connection," Fran replied. Blanco began looking in the drawers. As he reached in, he felt a hard object wrapped in a towel. Suddenly, he was struck across the back with a wooden chair, breaking it to pieces and bringing him to one knee.

She scrambled to pick up a leg from the broken chair, swinging it wildly, connecting with his shoulder and back. Blanco tried to block the blows with his arms over his head and rushed her in an attempt to push her down, but she was too fast, continually hitting him. Enduring multiple bashes, he got back to his feet as her onslaught continued relentlessly. Her assault was vicious as she screamed, "I love him! No one will hurt him while I'm alive!"

Blanco reached for his gun, and with a swing like Willie Mays, she whacked it out of his hand, sending it across the room. She attacked his legs, bringing him down again, bombarding him with hard shots. Blanco was weakening and fell into unconsciousness. She jumped to her feet and retrieved a roll of butcher twine from the kitchenette, binding his hands and feet behind his back. She put a pair of socks in his mouth and sat opposite him on the floor.

"What are we going to do now, Detective?" Fran taunted.

Then there was a knock on the door. It was David, "Fran! Are you alright? I heard screams! Are you OK? Fran! Open the door!" She got up from the floor and went to the door as the knocking continued until she opened it.

"Thank God you are OK," David said. She came out into the hall, closing the door behind her.

"I'm just so frightened, David. I became so anxious and hysterical with frustration that I screamed," she explained.

She went to him as he opened his arms, holding her closely as she cuddled into him. "It's OK, Fran, we are all scared. Come with me to my room; I'll make some tea. You can stay as long as you wish. Has Blanco come to you yet?"

"Blanco? Yes, he has come and gone a while ago."

French spent the day with his team covering 25 mansions. The reports suggested that Dominata likely hadn't been meeting for at least 10 years. He headed to the mansion to report to Detective Blanco.

William took charge after Eric's arrest, preparing trays of food to be sent to the guests' rooms. Not being a culinary whiz, he prepared finger sandwiches and salads.

Lester retired to his room to mourn his loss of Carol, while Simone and Claude went to her suite to plan what to do after all this was over. "Would you want to come to Florida with me?" Claude asked. "I've never been to Florida. That might be a good place to start."

Claude continued, "I never imagined that I would be wealthy and meet someone as beautiful as you, Simone."

"That's sweet, Claude," she said, snuggling next to him on the chaise lounge. "Have you wondered what we will receive?"

"I never really cared about money. I just tried to enjoy life, simply. I don't want to change that," Claude replied.

Simone expressed her disbelief, saying, "I still can't believe this is happening. All these deaths. It's a nightmare. This old man dies, a man we didn't know existed. Somehow we are related to him, and all this can be ours. Possibly. The frightfulness of these killings. Is it worth all these lives? It's blood money."

"You're right, Simone. We have to stay safe together until this plays out," Claude agreed. There was a knock on the door, and it was Marie with a tray cart. "Bring it in, please," Claude said. "Thank you."

Meanwhile, Lester was on his bed, staring up at the canopy, lost in thoughts of Carol.

Dr. Rojas entered the vestibule in search of Blanco, and Officer Chism offered to help. "Have you seen Detective Blanco?" Dr. Rojas inquired.

"I think that he was doing a room-to-room search, Doctor. I can go look for him, Sir," Officer Chism replied.

"That would be great, Officer Chism," Dr. Rojas said, and he turned, heading for the kitchen to start knocking on doors. He checked Joseph and William's rooms and then proceeded to Audrey's door. She answered, "Excuse me, Mam. Did Detective Blanco come by yet?"

"Yes, he did, Officer, about half an hour ago," Audrey replied.

"Did he say where he was going next?" Officer Chism asked.

"He would go to the right, Officer. All the rooms are in a row down the hall," Audrey informed him. He nodded and continued to Carmen and Anna's rooms. When he reached Fran's room, he knocked, and the door swung open. He called out, "Is anyone here? Hello!"

Blanco, who had been bound and unconscious, awoke upon hearing Officer Chism's voice. He struggled to make some noise and pushed his head into a nearby floor lamp, tipping it over just as Chism was about to leave. Startled, Chism turned to see what had caused the commotion. As he ventured further into the flat, he discovered Blanco on the floor.

"Detective! Are you alright?" Officer Chism rushed to the kitchenette, retrieved a knife, and used it to release Blanco from his bonds. Helping him to his feet, he asked, "What happened here, Sir?"

"Fran Geller attacked me. We must find her," Blanco replied urgently.

* * *

Fran was thinking, "I have to do something with Blanco." She told David, "Thank you for your concerns, but I have to go back to my flat."

"Are you sure that you don't want to stay here with me?" David asked.

"Yes, I'll be OK. Now," Fran replied. She left his room and returned to hers, only to find Blanco gone. Surprised, she hurriedly put on her shoes and ran out into the hall to the service staircase that led up to the bedrooms and down to the basement. The lights were still on as she descended into the depths of the mansion.

Meanwhile, Blanco gathered all his officers together. "We have to find Fran Geller. She attacked me, and she is responsible for most of the killings. Search everywhere. Chism, call the station for more help." They spread out and meticulously went through every room. Blanco instructed them, "Search the grounds; she has to be here somewhere. Go through the passages." Then he had a sudden realization. "The tunnels! Get the dogs," he shouted.

Officer French arrived amid the chaos and approached Blanco. "What's happening, Sir?"

"I was attacked by Fran Geller. She is missing, and we have to find her. Can you take a few officers down to the tunnels? I have a feeling that's where she is heading."

"Sure thing, Sir," French replied. Blanco had a great deal of respect for Officer French, seeing many similarities between them in terms of ambition, dedication, and going the extra mile on a case.

Blanco's body ached from the beating he had endured. Dr. Rojas was still on the scene and offered to take a look at his wounds. "Let me take a look at those wounds, Sam," he said.

"I have to find Fran Geller," Blanco insisted.

"Just a quick look," Dr. Rojas said, and they moved into the study. "She did quite a job on you. I may want some X-rays."

Blanco gritted his teeth in pain but was determined. "I have to settle this first, Doc."

"Go easy, Sam. You're pretty banged up," Dr. Rojas cautioned.

"Thanks, Doc," Blanco replied before heading off to the tunnels in search of Fran Geller.

* * *

Chapter Seventeen

Mr. Shwartzcoff pulled the tapestry bell for service, and David promptly appeared at the door. "You rang, Sir?" he inquired.

"I need to see the family regarding the will. Can you bring them to me?" Mr. Shwartzcoff requested.

"Yes, of course, Sir. Right away," David replied, swiftly moving to fulfill the task.

David proceeded to Simone's suite, where he knocked on the door, and Claude answered. "Excuse me, Sir. Mr. Shwartzcoff would like to request you and Ms. Geoffrey to come to his suite to discuss the will," David informed.

"We will be there shortly, David. Thank you," Claude acknowledged, conveying their readiness to comply.

Next, David went to Lester Coonz's door and knocked. Lester answered and received the same message. A few minutes later, the trio had gathered at Mr. Shwartzcoff's suite.

"Good evening. Please come in," Mr. Shwartzcoff greeted them, ushering them inside. "I have been instructed by my office to proceed as follows. So, please be seated as I, counsel for the Estate of Sir Andrew Van Cleese, present the last will and testament."

As they settled in their seats, Mr. Shwartzcoff began with the formal introduction, "I, Sir Andrew Van Cleese, being of sound mind..."

However, the trio was too eager to hear the content of the will and paid little attention to the preamble.

"First to my butler and dear friend, Eric Klaus, who has dedicated 50 years of his life to serving me and this house unquestionably, I leave 3 million dollars."

The three of them sat up in their seats, shocked by the unexpected amount. Claude couldn't help but comment, "3 million dollars? And he's in jail. How is that for karma?"

"My remaining funds of 25 million dollars, along with all of my real estate holdings, are to be shared equally among my brother Bernard's illegitimate children. May they use it to benefit the needy and live better lives than my brother did," Mr. Shwartzcoff announced.

"To my dedicated staff, I bequeath this Mansion to maintain and live in as a permanent part of my legacy, accompanied by a nest egg of $250,000.00 each," he continued.

Simone and Claude embraced each other with boundless joy. However, Lester's reaction was quite different. He broke down in tears, lamenting, "We could have had so much together. Oh Carol! Why? Why?" His grief was inconsolable.

Mr. Shwartzcoff assured them, "All the necessary paperwork is in order. I recommend that you seek the guidance of attorneys to help you navigate your newfound wealth. Good luck to you all. Now, I must meet with the staff to inform them of their good fortune." With those words, he exited the room.

In the meeting chamber below, Blanco and French were joined by two officers. One of the officers inquired, "She could be anywhere, Sir. Where should we begin our search?"

Blanco responded, "Send an officer to her room to retrieve a piece of her clothing, and let's bring in the dogs."

At the bottom of the service stairwell, Fran reached another door and pushed it open, revealing an enormous boiler room. Dominating the space were two colossal cylinders housing massive oil-fueled burners, nestled in a pit at the room's center. An intricate web of pipes crisscrossed the ceiling, while an expansive electrical panel adorned half of one wall. Spotting another door, Fran hurriedly crossed the room and dashed through it, finding herself in a tunnel with another ascending staircase.

As she made her way through the tunnel, Fran's ears caught the sound of voices ahead. She halted, recognizing Blanco's distinct tone. "We need the dogs," he declared. Fran's mind raced, wondering how Blanco had managed to free himself.

Panic surged through her, and Fran swiftly made the decision to retreat. She sprinted back to the staircase leading up to the door. Emerging at the top, she found herself facing an exit that led outside. It was the service entrance and delivery platform situated at the rear of the estate, with a lengthy driveway leading to the rear gate.

Hastily, Fran sought cover behind the shrubbery, her heart pounding with a mixture of fear and adrenaline. Beneath the gate, she discovered a narrow eighteen-inch gap, which she slid under, finally escaping the confines of the estate. Now alone, without money, identification, or belongings, she knew she had to distance herself from this place. Fran jogged westward, heading toward the heart of Newport, surrounded by imposing mansions, walls, fences, and gates.

Meanwhile, Mr. Shwartzcoff entered the kitchen to gather the staff. William and Joseph were engrossed in their preparations. Addressing them, Mr. Shwartzcoff requested, "Could you please assemble the staff? I need to read them Sir Andrew's will."

"Of course, Sir," Joseph replied. He walked over to the corner and pulled the tapestry strap to ring the bell. In a short while, all the staff members were gathered except for Fran. Concerned, they asked each other if anyone had seen her.

"Haven't you heard that the Police are looking for her? Seems she attacked Detective Blanco and disappeared," Carmen informed them.

"I hope she is OK," Marie added.

Mr. Shwartzcoff then presented the Will to the surprise and delight of all those present. They cheered, and David opened champagne for everyone, including Mr. Shwartzcoff, who raised a glass and smiled with them.

The staff celebrated their newfound wealth, dancing around the kitchen. Claude and Simone, overhearing the festivities, ventured into the vestibule in search of one of the staff members. Upon finding the kitchen and joining the merriment, they raised a toast with champagne.

Blanco headed up to the study to make arrangements for the release of Pierre LaMonte and inquire about the arrival time of the tracking dogs. Meanwhile, Officer French and his team continued searching for signs of Fran in the tunnels.

Eighty-six-year-old widow Penelope Hollbrooke pulled her Lincoln Town Car out of the garage, as she did every day, to drive down to the port and watch the boats coming and going. It brought her a sense of peace. However, on this particular day, a fly buzzed around her, distracting her. As she swatted at it, she inadvertently drove into Fran, who was jogging across the intersection. The impact sent Fran flying up onto the hood of Penelope's car before she rolled off and fell unconscious onto the street.

Panicked, Penelope got out of her car, screaming for help. Bystanders rushed to assist and called the police and an ambulance. Fran had sustained multiple contusions, head trauma, and was unconscious. The paramedics arrived, rushing her to Newport Hospital, where she was admitted and received medical treatment.

Pierre LaMonte pulled up the driveway of the Estate, got out of the cab, went in the front door through the vestibule, and into the kitchen, where the party was going on. When he entered, they all cheered and told him of their good fortune as the ladies surrounded him, welcoming his return.

Two police cars entered the driveway, each with two officers and one K-9. They entered the vestibule. Blanco met them and brought them down to the tunnels to meet Officer French. Officer Chism gave the handlers the shirt that belonged to Fran. The dogs were allowed to smell the garment and began barking and circling, going back and forth. Blanco said, "Okay, French, I'll be around."

At Newport Hospital, Fran, having no ID, was listed as Jane Doe. She had a concussion, a broken arm, a broken leg, three ribs, and was still unconscious. Penelope Hollbrooke wasn't taking it well, as she trembled and cried. "I feel so bad about that poor girl. I'm sorry, I didn't mean it. It was an accident, an accident."

Lester went to see Blanco in the study. "I guess we can all leave now that you know who your suspects are. Right? Detective."

"I think that you may be right, Mr. Coonz. I believe Mr. LaMonte was released also."

"Can't say it's been a pleasure, Detective. I'll be leaving in the morning."

"Good luck, Mr. Coonz."

Blanco got up and went towards the kitchen. Seeing Simone and Claude, he said, "Ms. Geoffrey, Mr. Abrams, I guess you can be on your way now. It seems we know who the culprits are. Congratulations, and good luck."

"Thank you, Detective. Our inheritance doesn't ease the awful occurrences here. This nightmare will haunt all of us for years to come," Simone said as she wiped tears from her eyes. Claude just nodded as they turned and left.

Turning around, Blanco was face to face with Pierre LaMonte. "So, Detective, where do we go from here?"

"We find Fran Geller, Mr. LaMonte. What can you tell me about her? It seems she was very fond of you."

"Francine and I were very close. She was special to me also, but no more than any of the ladies here."

"You must be quite a guy, Mr. LaMonte. Why do you think she would commit those acts, Mr. LaMonte?"

"I have no answer for that, Detective."

Down in the tunnels, Officer French and his team were following the dogs with no success. Until one dog was pulling away towards a smaller tunnel going back into the house. Following the dog to the staircase up and out to the rear of the Estate. "We have a scent, Officer French!"

Once outside, both dogs pulled and barked towards the back gate. "Get this opened," called Officer Grace. The dogs were barking and pulling to get through. Once opened, they were running down the road until they came to a stop at the location of the accident. "What happened here?" asked Officer French. "I have to call this in."

French went back to the Mansion to find Blanco. "The dogs found the scent and led us out the back gate of the Estate. They stopped at the corners of 12th Ave. and Cedar Street."

"Call the station and find out what happened there."

"Yes, Sir." French called Sergeant Syms. "Newport Police, can I help you?"

"Sergeant Syms, this is Officer French. I'm working with Detective Blanco on the Van Cleese case. Was there an incident at the corners of 12th Avenue and Cedar Street today?"

"Let me check." A pause. "Yes, there was an accident. A car collided with a pedestrian, an unidentified female. She was brought to Newport Hospital."

"Thank you, Sergeant." Rushing back to Blanco. "She's at Newport Hospital, Sir! Hit by a car."

"What? Let's go, French! Hurry!" They ran out to the big black Mercury, put the flasher on the roof, and headed to the hospital.

Doctors were working on Fran. They set her arm and leg, and did a CT scan of her head. She had a concussion and was semi-conscious. Blanco and French arrived and ran into the emergency room, asking at the desk for a young lady who was hit by a car.

"I'm sorry, Detective, but the doctors are attending to her as we speak."

"What's her condition right now?"

"I can't answer that. You'll have to speak with the doctors."

"We'll wait." Hours passed until anyone came out.

"Good evening, Detective, I'm Doctor Cambridge. I'm attending to Ms. Doe. She has no ID. She is in guarded condition with multiple injuries. She is semi-conscious and not responding at this time. We have to wait and see what develops."

"Her name is Francine Geller, Doctor. She is wanted in connection with a very serious case."

"Well, I'm sorry, Detective, she is not able to speak to you at this time, and I assure you she is unable to leave any time soon."

"Thank you, Doctor. I'll be back tomorrow." Blanco brought Officer French back to the Mansion. "I guess we can start wrapping this up, French. You have been a great asset to this case. I certainly will let Captain Lockhart know about it."

"Thank you, Detective." Blanco went home to Christina.

Lester was all packed and ready to go when Joseph knocked, announcing breakfast at 9 am. Lester smiled. "Well, this is it," he said, heading down to the dining room.

Claude and Simone showered together, starting their day in erotic harmony. They heard Joseph's announcement as they dressed. "We can pack later," Claude said, and they too headed down to breakfast.

• • •

Mr. Shwartzcoff had a bit of a hangover. He hadn't had that much champagne in a long time. He got out of bed as Joseph informed him of breakfast from the door. He showered and joined the others at the table.

Simone said, "This has been an experience of a lifetime. Some of us can walk away to enjoy a new beginning. Sadly, those lost in this week of turmoil can't. I will always carry that sadness in my heart." Lester wiped away some tears. "This has changed my life in so many ways. I have never felt such emotion in my life. Losing Carol, even though we were together for a short time, meant more to me than any amount of money. She will fill my dreams with happiness."

Claude stood and said, "Before coming here, my life was good. I had nothing and didn't miss it. I was content day by day, enjoying simple pleasures. This has brought me to a new level. Meeting Simone is a treasure I could never have imagined. I have been living a fantasy this week with her, and the added bonus of this inheritance only adds to the illusion. My heart breaks for those we lost here, bringing a darkness to our bounty. May they all rest peacefully knowing that their assailants will be punished."

They ate and thanked Mr. Shwartzcoff, leaving the room. All the police had gone, and the staff was already working on a new day and a new life.

Blanco woke up next to Christina. "This case has been one of my toughest, and it's not over. I have one suspect in custody, the other in the hospital."

"You need to relax, Sam. Put it all aside for now," she said, lying next to him with her hand on his chest, gently rubbing. "Calm down." Her hand slowly moved lower, arousing him. She caressed and took him into her hand, massaging slowly. He looked at her, smiling. "Now that you put it that way." They made passionate and tender love. Every time he was with her, he felt like he was dreaming. "I think after this case, I'm calling it quits. Why would I want to miss a single moment with you?"

"I love the sound of that," she replied. Later, he took a shower. "I have to go for a while, sweetheart."

"I'll fix you a nice dinner, Sam. I love you." They kissed, and he headed off to the hospital.

Upon entering the hospital, he approached the front desk and asked for Francine Geller's room. "I'll see if the doctor can come out."

"Is there a problem?" Blanco inquired.

"I'll get the doctor, sir," the receptionist replied. Blanco took a seat and waited. After about half an hour, the doctor emerged. "My apologies for the delay, detective. I was with another patient."

"No problem, doctor. So, how is our Ms. Geller?"

"Well, it appears that Ms. Geller doesn't know who she is. I believe she has retrograde amnesia. She is unable to recall any past information. This condition is a result of severe head injuries, and there is no way of knowing how long it will last. Her memory may return over time, or it may not return at all."

"May I see her?"

"Only if you don't pressure her."

"No problem, I'll be brief."

Up in the room, Blanco remained silent. Fran was resting with her eyes closed. Her arm and leg were in casts, with her leg elevated in a sling above the bed. Her head was wrapped in bandages, with oxygen tubes in her nose and mouth. He stood there, observing her, when she opened her eyes and looked at him.

"Hello, Francine. Remember me?" he asked. There was no reaction, just a cold stare, and then she drifted back to sleep. Blanco quietly left the room.

Once a week, he returned to find her physically improving, but the blank stare continued, and when he said, "Hello, Francine, remember me?" there was absolutely no reaction. He went to see Doctor Cambridge. "So what's the prognosis, Doctor?"

"Detective, physically she is healing nicely. Her mental state is not. She has extensive brain damage, and she may never recover."

Simone and Claude were down in Miami, enjoying their new-found wealth and planning to travel the world together. Lester was back in Chicago, still heartbroken over Carol. He tried to keep busy with his real estate business, but his heart wasn't in it. His loneliness was making him bitter. No amount of money can buy happiness.

Pierre and the staff at the Mansion were content for the moment. They all moved into their own suites out of the servants' quarters. Pierre still prepared meals, and all the chores were kept up to par. Extra activities continued after hours with the ladies and Pierre, while the butlers went out on their own endeavors.

Blanco and Christina spent a lot of time together, except that Blanco was plagued by not closing the case. Eric Klaus confessed to the crimes and was sentenced to twenty-five years to life in prison with no chance of parole. After working all of his life, he was now a millionaire in a cell in the state penitentiary.

Then, Francine Geller was transferred to a state psychiatric institution with Retrograde Amnesia, making her unable to stand trial for the murders she committed. Blanco went to see her monthly. Entering her room, he would say, "I'm back, Francine. How are you today?" She would just stare blankly at him. "Do you remember Pierre, Francine?" No reactions. Month after month. "Hello, Francine, I'm back. Do you remember Carol, or Nancy, or maybe Linda and Thomas? How about Trey Wilson?" No reaction. After he left, she would simply smile...